Praise for *Tell Me I'm an Artist*

"Anyone who has ever tried to do meaningful work in spite of a growing suspicion that nothing matters will find a home in this hilarious, heart-piercing book, and a memorable companion in its young but wise narrator. Chelsea Martin is a born storyteller."
　　　　　　　　　—EMILY GOULD, author of *Perfect Tunes*

"Overflowing with humor and honesty, *Tell Me I'm an Artist* interrogates the life of the artist from an engrossingly contemporary angle. It's a monument to the big and small ways in which we craft our notions of artistry, and to Chelsea Martin's dazzling skill as a writer."
　　　　　　　　　　　　　　　—ALEXANDRA KLEEMAN,
　　　　　　　　　　　author of *Something New Under the Sun*

"Portrait of the artist as a broke and brilliant, hungry and funny young woman, Chelsea Martin's *Tell Me I'm an Artist* is an acutely felt and beautifully rendered depiction of all the absurd, messy, complicated layers of trying to make things, a story not only of ambition and yearning but also of triumph and loving."
　　　　　　　　　—LYNN STEGER STRONG, author of *Want*

"*Tell Me I'm an Artist* perfectly renders the high drama of artistic procrastination—the anxiety, the doubt, the hesitation, the momentary flights of confidence, the will I/won't I. It's warm, it's deadpan, it's absurd. I loved this book."　　　　　　—HALLE BUTLER,
　　　　　　　　　　　　　　　author of *The New Me*

"Deft and exquisite and singular, Chelsea Martin's *Tell Me I'm an Artist* urges us to consider what we owe—a lot or a little or zilch—to our families, our friends, our ambitions, ourselves. Funny and

crushing, lithe and deep, this novel is that rare combination of pleasure and profundity, a portrait of the artist as a work in progress."
—SHARMA SHIELDS, author of *The Cassandra*

"Chelsea Martin has quietly become one of our most prolific and hardworking contemporary writers—always fresh yet understated, calmly insightful, mumbling profundity so casually that one questions whether she recognizes its brilliance. *Tell Me I'm an Artist* is another home run, impossible not to devour immediately. Never before have I read such a precise encapsulation of the underaddressed ennui of family dysfunction and mother-daughter relationships."
—DARCIE WILDER, author of *literally show me a healthy person*

"In *Tell Me I'm an Artist*, Chelsea Martin tells my favorite kind of love story—that between an artist and her work. She explores how crippling self-doubt, desperation, and abject terror are all threads of the creative process, tangled up with euphoria, self-discovery, and transcendence."   —HALLIE BATEMAN, author of *Directions*

"The funniest, smartest, Chelsea-est novel you could only dream of. I savored every page, and when I finished, I wanted to begin again. In the forms of lists, internet searches, fragments, and impeccable pacing, Chelsea Martin tackles the notion of being an 'artist' in this unpredictable and colorful novel for our times."
—CHLOE CALDWELL, author of *The Red Zone: A Love Story*

TELL ME I'M AN ARTIST

TELL ME I'M AN ARTIST

A NOVEL

CHELSEA MARTIN

SOFT SKULL   NEW YORK

First Soft Skull edition: 2022

Library of Congress Cataloging-in-Publication Data
Names: Martin, Chelsea, 1986– author.
Title: Tell me I'm an artist : a novel / Chelsea Martin.
Other titles: Tell me I am an artist
Description: First Soft Skull edition. | New York : Soft Skull, 2022.
Identifiers: LCCN 2021059369 | ISBN 9781593767211 (hardcover) |
    ISBN 9781593767228 (ebook)
Classification: LCC PS3613.A77783 T45 2022 | DDC 813/.6—dc23
LC record available at https://lccn.loc.gov/2021059369

Jacket design by www.houseofthought.io
Book design by Wah-Ming Chang

Published by Soft Skull Press
New York, NY
www.softskull.com

Printed in the United States of America

10 9 8 7 6 5 4 3 2 1

TELL ME I'M AN ARTIST

I hadn't seen *Rushmore*. That was the premise. I knew very little about it, aside from some visuals of the characters that popped up on TV or online. I knew that Jason Schwartzman wore a red beret, for example. I knew that Bill Murray went to a pool. I wanted to remake the film based on other people's memories of it, strangers, hopefully a lot of them. A collective understanding of *Rushmore*, but researched and produced by me, with all creative decisions being mine. Also, I'd play all the parts.

I was nervous and started to trip over my words as I described this project to my classmates. They don't tell you how much public speaking is involved in making art. But it was an important part of the process, I was assured. Very few ideas seemed cool after I heard myself talk about them.

I was lucky to be at art school among these bright, creative minds. But I was here, too, so I was one of the bright, creative minds advertised to other bright creative minds as one of the reasons they should be here. Which worried me. I didn't feel like a bright, creative mind. I wondered if we had all bought into a self-referential pyramid scheme because we badly wanted to believe that we could be considered, to someone, a bright, creative mind.

"I guess I am interested in creating an experience of this film that more closely represents what culture remembers about it," I said, trying to sum up my project quickly so I could sit down. I dropped my notebook on the table in front of me to indicate that I was done talking.

"Are you planning to shoot digitally or on film?" someone asked after a few moments of silence. He spoke slowly, and broke eye contact with me to look out the window halfway through his question. This was the structured discourse the college pamphlets had promised me. Skipping P.E. one day in high school two years before to sit behind the maintenance shed and look at art school pamphlets, I'd read about the supportive community, gorgeous facilities, and renowned professors that would change my artistic practice, and my life, forever. And now here I was being challenged to grow by the brightest creative minds in the nation.

"Digital," I said.

Would you necessarily know if your life was changing? Would you know if you had reached a corner, turned it, and were now headed in a different direction?

"Oh okay. I was gonna say, shooting in film might actually be really cool because the quality of film is much richer than digital, and would lend itself to a feeling of remove from the original movie. It's more expensive, obviously, but I think it would be worth the extra cost."

"Yeah, that's a good point," I said. I planned to remake *Rushmore* for as close to free as possible.

There were no other questions about my project. No other feedback. Which was good, because then another student stood up to present their idea and everyone stopped looking at me.

In the front corner of class, I noticed a wooden broom standing on its straw bristles at an angle I found pleasant and soothing (though I was simultaneously aware that those were absurd things to feel about a broom). I wondered if the broom was set there intentionally to please and soothe me, or to make me aware of my ability to be pleased and soothed by broom placement. Maybe it was someone's left-behind art project from another class. Or, alternately, maybe it was not art at all, but the work of a careless (or overworked) janitor. If it was left by a janitor, but still caused me to think about all the same things it would have if an artist had set it up, would it not be art? Maybe both could be true, and the janitor who left it there had artistic intentions about it. Maybe the artistic intention of the janitor was to make art students think about the invisible people employed to work for them. Maybe it was supposed to make art students feel guilty for the way they might subconsciously judge janitors as "care-less" and then, as if their subconscious minds were aware of the shit-tiness of their judgments and wanted to prove to their conscious minds that they (the subconscious minds) had nuanced and sensi-tive ways of looking at things, added "or overworked" in there, you know, to let you (the art student's conscious mind) know they're on the right side of history. I then noticed there was a small pile of dust and dirt next to the broom, a little brown pyramid like cartoon dust sweepings. This, to me, felt too on the nose, too convenient, proof that the broom was an intentional artistic gesture meant to bring awareness to the classist assumptions within the viewer and pit their conscious and unconscious minds against each other. Oh, it was art, undoubtedly.

My classmates presented their own film project ideas one after another. The assignment was a self-portrait, to be completed over the course of the whole semester. Everyone else's projects seemed to be pretty literal interpretations of the assignment. Suz had convinced me I could do whatever I wanted and call it a self-portrait.

"You overestimate the intellectual rigor of our peer group," she had said.

Dirk would film himself coming out to his parents over Easter brunch. Larissa would film herself telling the story of her sexual abuse one sentence at a time over the course of the semester. Cox would paint herself in period blood and apologize to her unborn siblings.

I felt sympathetic nervousness for no reason as Suz looked over her notes at the podium. Suz was probably the only person who would think of me if asked for a list of friends' names. Her film would be made up of found footage of her mom from the eighties. In this piece, Suz wanted to talk about the otherness her mom felt as an immigrant, and how that feeling of otherness can be passed down. The film was powerful already, before its existence, as she spoke about it. She had a way of making assignments feel like they were conceived around an idea she already had and was going to do anyway, whereas I always felt assignments were designed to make me less and less sure of what art was.

Professor Herrera assigned staggered due dates for us over the last four sessions of the semester. Mine would be on the final day.

After class, I walked into the bright hallway and waited for Suz.

"Dude, Cox is always making art about her mom's miscarriages," Suz said. "Like, literally every class I've had with her it's come up. That, or her dead fetal twin."

I laughed and looked around to make sure Cox wasn't in earshot.

"Like, we get it, you have a family," I said. "It's like Jemma and her obsession with making her work look like it was an accident. You're in art school. You can admit you make art."

"I'm into that though," Suz said. "People are so obsessed with art being this grandiose, time-consuming, expensive thing. I like that she's countering that."

"Right," I said.

Suz pulled a cigarette out of her trench coat and held it unlit between her fingers. "Want to come over and sit on my roof?"

The *Rushmore* thing felt like an exciting new direction for my art. I came to art school with a portfolio full of portraits, and that is mostly what I continued to do once I got there. Portraits of my friends. Portraits of people I wanted to be friends with, who I painted as a way into their consciousness. "Can I take a few photos of you for reference for a painting?" I would say as a way to initiate contact with people I wanted to talk to. I joked with Suz that I wanted a record of the people I knew so future historians would know that I knew people. It's not a funny joke unless you think being lonely and desperate is funny. Being lonely and desperate is only funny if you know there is a way out.

There were a few other students in my year who worked in portraiture. I cringed when they hung their work on the walls. The faces they painted were meaningless to me, so flat and void of the tension I saw looking at a face in real life. I moved to self-portraiture, forcing people to look at representations of me closely and then talk about my face with me. It felt artistically interesting to spend twelve hours trying to capture the puffiness under my eyes. And when I was done, the puffs represented the time I had spent painting them, and the puffs under my real eyes were caused by the puffs I had painted, a circular system. But the critiques were always focused on technique rather than the story I was trying to tell in paint. "Try more blue in the shadow shapes." "This feels a little overworked. I'd like to see you to loosen up."

I took Experimental Film to get out of my head a bit, try a different medium, and because Suz was taking it. When Professor Herrera told us we would be making experimental self-portraits, I considered dropping the class. I could see if it wasn't too late to get into Glass Blowing. But Suz told me I could interpret the assignment loosely and do pretty much whatever I wanted, and that there would be other small projects throughout the semester as well. It seemed like Suz wanted me there. So I stayed.

Anything could be a self-portrait, like Suz said. My choices and preferences and interpretations would be present in anything I chose to do. I could make a film about literally anything and it would still be a reflection of me. I picked a topic randomly, something I thought had nothing to do with me, a topic I didn't know anything about: the 1998 Wes Anderson film *Rushmore*. I wasn't sure what it would say about me in the end. Maybe something about memory. Or how I experience other peoples' experiences of popular culture. Or the experience of existing in a world where things exist that have nothing to do with me. Maybe I would be surprised at what would be revealed about me.

Most of us considered leaving art school after the first year. The education we were getting mostly consisted of identifying the limits of our creativity and the huge gaps in our self-understanding, and detailed insight about our professors' bodies of work, which we were shown on projectors on the last day of class, always, like a treat, like they had been waiting the whole semester to reveal to us how amazing they were.

"Beautiful work," a professor might say during critique. "Just really jarring." Then the professor would stand in front of our work thoughtfully, turn around, and say, "What does everyone else think?" It was the kind of discourse that didn't seem worth paying thousands of dollars for. But here we all were, paying for it. Here we were signing up for another semester of it. What else could we do? Go back to our hometowns and be ceramic teachers at local guilds? Get jobs at indie bookstores and do art in our free time, continuing to take advantage of the college's free lectures and art shows and shuttle buses and even studio space if we were sneaky enough? It made suspiciously too much sense.

"I should move to New York," Suz often said. "The art scene here is not what I expected. It's like there's no ambition."

I never considered leaving school. I understood the education I was getting was of questionable quality and limited practicality, but I loved college life. I loved the deadlines and critiques and readings. I loved having access to the studios at any time in the night or day. I loved my apartment, a tiny, drafty second-floor studio I had all to myself, paid for by loans with interest levels I was not taught to understand. I left supplies out, sketchbooks open, and finished work pinned to the walls. I played music from my laptop in my tiny kitchen while I made quesadillas in the microwave with American cheese slices. I ate at a step stool on the floor next to the foot of my bed, a setup I referred to as the Formal Dining Room. Every morning I walked 1.5 miles to school carrying a huge portfolio, often in the rain, thinking, *No one has ever been so lucky.*

"What do you think of my film project idea?" Suz said. We were walking from where she parked her car to her apartment a few blocks over. "I don't normally make work about my family. Does it sound cheesy?"

"I mean, everyone always loves your work. You have nothing to worry about."

"I'm asking your opinion."

"My opinion is that everyone always loves your work, including me. It's going to be great."

I could tell the compliment disappointed her. She was looking for something deeper from me, perhaps something rooted in art theory. A reference to some other artwork, or an awareness of the symbolism her idea might reflect. This was how she talked in class, relating our peers' work to art movements of the past, seeing layers of meaning in smears of charcoal, going on and on about the texts we were assigned to read. My own artistic interpretations were shallow and simplistic by comparison. "That hand looks too small for that body," is a critique I might offer. Or, "I'd like to see more red."

"I'm going to cut the footage of my mom with other things, obviously. I want to work with the idea of my mom as a woman in a society that hates women, and with my own role in participating in misogyny."

"Oh, wow," I said.

I liked watching Suz's brain work, even if I usually couldn't follow its path. It was interesting to see how quickly she could get from Point A (a pen drawing of a house on fire, for example) to Point B (the fragility of humanity) without making any huge logical leaps. I always thought she must have already had the fragility of humanity on her mind and was looking everywhere for new ways to think about it. The idea of approaching art—or life—with your own agenda, rather than waiting to see what it told you, seemed original to me. And the idea of pondering the fragility of humanity in your spare time seemed hilarious.

We turned onto Suz's street, which was lined with lush green trees. These kinds of tree-lined streets of historic buildings always gave me a jolt of realization that I was living in San Francisco, a place where millions of different kinds of people have lived, cared for, and built communities.

Small cities like Lodi, where I grew up, offered only sameness and emptiness. Green lawns, cars baking in the sun, hundreds of miles of sidewalk that rarely got used.

Not that San Francisco was a utopia or anything. There was garbage in the streets and human feces in doorways and it was pretty likely your bike would get stolen if you left it on a bike rack overnight without using two sixty-dollar U-locks. But people cared about the city, and it made the city feel alive. People put flowerpots on their stoops. People opened coffee shops and named them after the neighborhood they were in. Sometimes you'd see a fragile new tree planted on one of the sidewalks, and everyone, even the street drunks, would be careful not to run into it.

I took up space in this miraculous city. Thinking about it felt electric.

We put our things down inside her apartment and then went through the kitchen window to the roof. We sat on plastic chairs, took sweaters out of our bags and spread them out over our laps so we wouldn't get cold or sunburned. You could never tell in San Francisco. We were quiet for a few minutes, a comfortable, relaxed silence I didn't experience with many people, and then Suz pulled a book from her bag and started reading it. I took out my sketchbook and a candid photograph of myself on Christmas when I was eleven, sitting among unopened presents under a Christmas tree looking displeased, and started drawing my own chubby preadolescent face on a clean new sheet.

I walked to the Muni from Suz's apartment, took the Muni to BART, and BART to Sixteenth, and then walked to my apartment.

I walked to the kitchen and turned on the kettle. I got a good deal on my studio apartment, but it would have been cheaper if I had found something with roommates. With the school loan that came through at the start of the semester, I'd have enough money to get through until summer if I didn't buy any more art supplies or books or hot dogs from street vendors. And living alone had been my fantasy ever since my freshman-year roommate flung open the curtain while I was sitting on the shower floor crying and yelled at me for purportedly using her hand towel.

That's what the loans were for, I reasoned: allowing me to pretend that living alone was a luxury someone like me deserved.

When the kettle whistled, I poured water into a Cup O' Noodles, filling it to the thin Styrofoam line.

I liked Cup O' Noodles because the noodles didn't get soggy. I felt that living alone allowed me to appreciate feats of food engineering while not knowing what exactly was meant by the term *food engineering*.

The *Rushmore* project could be a way of taking ownership of unknowable things. *Rushmore* itself wasn't unknowable since I could easily watch it and "know." But it represented all the unknowable things, things unknowable simply because there was not enough time to know everything within a lifetime. Just because I didn't know what something was didn't mean I couldn't have an opinion about it. Maybe not knowing made my opinion more interesting, because it was based only on my preconceptions, my personal interests, my understanding of the world.

When I finally started eating the noodles, they were, in fact, a little soggy. Oh, to see the look on my face when I realized how wrong I'd been about food engineering!

I turned on a clip of a 1995 episode of *SNL*, turned off all the lights, and ate by the light of my laptop screen.

I heard my phone vibrate and I took it out of my bag.

It was a text from Mom: *have u talked to jenny?*

I texted: *not for weeks why?*

Mom: *Can you please call her and tell her to call.me*

My mom was always doing this: asking me for information about Jenny's whereabouts or schedule, or trying to get me to lecture her about her shitty attitude or what time was appropriate to be coming home or whatever, as if I had more insight into and control over her daily life than my mom had living with her.

Jenny and I rarely talked outside of me telling her something Mom told me to tell her, and yet Mom apparently thought that since we were sisters we had sisterly insight into each other's lives, secret sister conversations in which we opened up, spoke quietly about deep truths, blathered about our common love for our mother, etc.

But telling Mom I wasn't close with Jenny and never had a desire to talk to her would be taken as a sign of my ungratefulness, proof of my inability to be a willing participant in a family that often forgot my birthday. It was not a battle I always wanted to fight.

"I'm not your middleman," I would sometimes say.

"Oh, right. You don't want to be part of this family. I guess I forgot," Mom would say.

But this time I thought: Whatever.

I texted Mom: *sure*

I texted Jenny: *call mom*

"Have you really never seen *Rushmore*?"

Suz was eating rice crackers and color-correcting photographs of her paintings on her laptop. Sunlight shone in from the window onto her skin, catching little flecks of her hair and landing all over the clean and empty surfaces in her room: windowsills, contemporary desk, teak side table, hardwood floor, my overnight bag, spilling over with the dirty laundry I planned on wearing the next day.

I prepared my *Rushmore* project Craigslist post on the floor beside her bed. The last time I posted on Craigslist, I was giving away a box of denim scraps that I had found in the Free Pile on campus. I'd thought I could use them for something and never did. Two different people wanted the box of denim scraps, so I told them whoever came and got it first could have it. The first lady came and got it within an hour. The second guy rang my buzzer at 1:00 a.m. and was pissed I didn't have the denim scraps anymore. He told me he had driven fifty-five miles for the denim scraps. He waited in my apartment entryway to see what I had to say about that. "I'm sorry," I had said, though in fact I was the opposite of sorry. That he would show up at my apartment so late, and, after seeing I was female and alone, yell at me about something that was already done made me happy I couldn't give him the denim scraps. I hoped he never saw a denim scrap again in his life.

"I bet you are sorry," he had said, standing menacingly in my doorway for a few seconds before stomping away.

This time, I would not invite people to show up at my apartment. I would set up meetings on campus, during daylight hours, when there would be witnesses.

"No," I said to Suz. "Have you?"

"Of course," she said. "It seems like something you would be into. Have you watched Wes Anderson's other films?"

"I saw *The Royal Tenenbaums* a while ago. It was okay," I said.

"It's interesting you would pick such an iconic filmmaker for this project," she said. "People have such strong opinions about him that they'll most certainly bring with them to your work. It's almost like you're challenging people to notice their own preconceived ideas."

"True," I said. "How does this sound?"

I read to her from my screen. "Looking for subjects to be interviewed about Wes Anderson's movie *Rushmore* for a school project. No pay but it probably won't take longer than twenty minutes for an interview and I'd be super grateful."

"Don't say the film's name because then people might rewatch it before they talk to you and that would defeat the purpose of it being their memory of the film, right?" Suz said.

I nodded and pressed backspace a bunch of times.

"Looking for subjects to be interviewed about film for a school project. No pay."

"Hmm. I think saying 'school' makes it sound amateur. Try to make it sound like it might be on TV or something."

"Really?" I said.

"I mean, they'll never know." She moved her face close to her screen and pressed some keys aggressively. I looked back at my own screen, trying to feel something profound about the fact that we were both looking into small objects containing large swaths of our lives, but it didn't feel like such a big deal.

"Looking for volunteer subjects to be interviewed on the subject of film for an upcoming documentary," I said.

"Yep. Perfect."

I woke up to a voicemail from my mom, and I waited to listen to the message while Suz was in the shower. In her message she said that Jenny's ex, Lucas, had found out Jenny was dating a seventeen-year-old named Antonio (he also happened to be Lucas's cousin) who worked at GameStop, and he had come to the house and was yelling and throwing things on the porch and threatening to turn Jenny in for statutory, saying he was going to get custody over their baby, Brian. My mom had called the police since he was causing a disturbance and the police said they could arrest him for being drunk and disorderly but then they didn't for some reason. Afterward Jenny had walked to her friend Katie's house, leaving Brian with my mom, and since then Jenny hadn't been home. My mom had the weekend off but when Monday came around she'd left Brian with a neighbor none of us knew very well while she went to work. Mom wanted to know could I please call her back with ideas of what to do with Brian? She was worried Lucas would try to abduct Brian from this neighbor's house. And also did I know anyone who might have Antonio's number because it was possible Jenny was with him?

"Do you want to grab coffee?" Suz said, emerging from the steamy bathroom. "I don't have class till ten."

"Sure," I said. I started collecting my things and dropping them into my backpack.

It's important to surround yourself with people you want to be more like. My friend Lindsay's grandma, Carol, once said this to me. She said you become like those who are nearest to you, even if you don't want to. The way she said it made me think it was something she had seen on an embroidered pillow, but for some reason it stuck with me. *I don't want to be anything like anyone I know*, I thought. *I should get away from them before it is too late.* Moving to San Francisco was a good opportunity to start over, to choose cool people to be around, to avoid anyone who might lead me down a dark path. I still kept a distance from almost everyone. These people weren't the people I wanted to be like, either, it turned out. But Suz was different. I'd tunnel into her skull and *Being John Malkovich* myself to her brain if I could.

Would this be a good time, my inner monologue said, *to show you my presentation about the many aspects of your terrible personality you refuse to improve?*

I stood in Suz's doorway holding my bike against the side of the building, waiting for Suz to tie up her boots. I dropped my phone into the largest compartment of my backpack to fall beneath my overnight clothes.

We walked three blocks to Blue Bottle Coffee. I reasoned it would be okay to spend $2.25 on a small cup this one time.

It had rained a lot overnight. The city was gray and moist, and we had to walk single file on the inner part of the sidewalk so we wouldn't get splashed by passing cars as they hit the large pools of water in the streets. I felt so lucky.

I had made it through my first year of college without really making friends. Sometimes I would go to dorm parties if the RA told me about them. Or I would go to the RA-hosted movie nights at the dorms and accidentally laugh only at times that other people did not laugh. Or sometimes someone would do yoga near me in the common area while I watched *House Hunters* and did my drawing homework and then a third person would come in and use the window glass to trace a sketch onto nice paper and it would feel like I was living in a photo collage scene out of those art school promotional pamphlets I loved so much.

In the second week of classes in my first semester of my second year of college on a break during Painting II, Suz asked me if I'd like to come over to her apartment after class to watch *The Conversation*. It was about surveillance, she said. A classic. She hadn't seen it in years.

She often complimented my drawings during critique, but we had never talked outside of class. The invitation was as natural as if we'd been hanging out all our lives. Her long, shiny black hair lay starkly against her neon-yellow peacoat as she smoked a cigarette. She said she had borrowed the DVD from the library. We could sit on her roof afterward and smoke weed. She gestured wildly with the hand she held the cigarette with, and smoke twirled around her like a magic potion.

"Sure," I said.

I tried to come up with some reason she would have picked me. My paintings never garnered much attention from anyone, and my comments were limited to a style of backhanded compliment I developed just for painting classes that allowed me to be honest with my classmates (participation was mandatory) while still being able to perceive myself as a nice person.

"I like how you use paints straight out of the tube rather than mixing your own colors," I might say. "It reminds me of a Paint By Numbers."

I followed Suz home after class and we watched the movie in her dark bedroom, neither of us saying anything, like we'd been friends forever. I'd expected to be bored by an "old classic," and I was at first, but soon became gripped by Gene Hackman's character's journey surveilling a young couple in trouble and trying to find a way to save them.

After the movie we climbed through floral kitchen curtains to the roof and drank vodka sodas she had made in a glass pitcher.

"People think having the internet and access to unlimited information makes them more informed and engaged with the world, but the opposite of that is true," she said.

"Hm," I said, trying to understand how that could be true.

"The internet makes us worse at listening, less engaged, less accountable. We think it can give us everything, that everything is searchable and knowable and that access to limitless information is a net gain."

"Ah," I said. "So true." I felt like I had watched a different film than Suz had. I hadn't been thinking about the internet at all.

"But even with all the information in the world, even with concrete conversations pulled directly from life, you could still be wrong about what they mean, and your wrongness could have any number of consequences."

"But the Gene Hackman character knows he could be wrong, I think. At least he knows he is part of the problem. He knows his job is evil and he does it anyway."

"And I think we do that, too. We willingly participate in our own surveillance. We put all our photos on Flickr and Facebook and think no one would ever be interested enough to rummage through our lives."

We exchanged phone numbers, and Suz put a smirking emoji next to my name because she said that's what my face looked like. I was flattered by the suggestion that I was someone she had noticed things about.

"See, you're doing it," she said. I put my hand over my face, embarrassed to be so happy.

Mom texted: *Did u get my voicemail? Can u come get Brian please? I need help*

What am I supposed to do w Brian? I texted.

I wanted to text: *I'm 90 miles away and have no car and I resent being asked to leave college and take care of a baby in a manner that suggests I am somehow responsible for this baby's health and well-being when I have spent years distancing myself from Jenny precisely because she takes advantage of everyone who tries to help her,* but I didn't text that.

I texted: *I have class*

I wanted to text: *Why doesn't Jenny just stop seeing the GameStop dude and figure out childcare for her own kid? You're enabling her by making this your problem to figure out.*

I thought about how my face looked while texting my mom. I felt myself furrowing slightly and quickly unfurrowed, overcorrecting momentarily into a happily surprised expression. I looked across the coffee shop table at Suz, who was flipping through a magazine called *Elephant.*

Thx ur so helpful as always, Mom texted.

Jenny had thought about adoption. She'd looked through forms filled out by hopeful couples, read letters from them about how much they would love and care for Brian, if given the opportunity. I was still in high school and was grateful no one asked my opinion about the situation. I didn't have one. I couldn't imagine bringing a person into the world. I couldn't imagine caring for or loving one. I also couldn't imagine giving one away, letting the world have its way with them without my supervision.

There was one couple Jenny liked a lot. They lived in Sacramento. They spoke of private school, tutors, trips to the husband's parents' house in Spain. The husband was a doctor; the wife ran a small pickle company that didn't take up much of her time. They had an inground pool in the backyard of the large, beautiful house they owned. Jenny's astonishment was misinterpreted as fear, and they immediately offered to have the pool filled in for safety. She took paperwork home to look over. She cried a lot about it.

I imagined Brian growing up and summoning the courage to find us, his biological family, to see for himself who we were. I imagined the relief he'd feel for how things had turned out, how lucky he had been not to grow up here. I imagined him shuddering at the idea of how close he had been to having a life like ours, faded denim, cigarettes bought in cartons, no pool. I imagined Jenny asking him for money. To get the power turned back on and a few groceries, she'd tell him. He'd go home, make an appointment with his therapist, discuss the pity he'd felt.

But Jenny got scared. She didn't want Brian growing up knowing there was at least one person in the world who didn't want him. She couldn't bring herself to do that. It was a gesture of love to hold him captive in this rotting family.

My mom and I said we understood, and that we supported her, that her choice was a good choice.

"Don't worry," Mom said. "Family sticks together. We'll all raise that baby."

"We're here for you," I said. "Whatever you need."

I said that.

For the day of my Craigslist interviews, I reserved a room across the street from the main campus in what could conceivably be an office building. I was trying to continue the illusion that this was a professional project and not something I didn't want to do for a class I probably shouldn't have taken. On the big whiteboard at the front of class, I wrote, *Room reserved 1/26/11 10–2pm Joelle Berry*. I clipped my notes to a clipboard and looked over the list of questions I had written the night before.

Have you seen the movie? Can you describe the plot? Who are the main characters? Do you remember any specific dialogue? What was the mood of the movie? What do the characters look like? Where does the movie take place? What is the climax of the movie? What is the motivation of each of the characters? What happens at the end? What made you watch it in the first place? Did you watch it in the theater? Did you rent it from a Redbox outside of 7-Eleven and watch it alone in your apartment? Did it leave an impression on you? Were there any plot holes?

My first interviewee said, "Why didn't you mention *Rushmore* in the ad if that's all you want to talk about? I could have told you I'd never seen it." He seemed angry, and I held back embarrassed tears while I tried to think of something to say that wouldn't make me look like an idiot.

It hit me what a monumentally stupid idea this was. It felt like realizing you're wrong in the middle of an argument. I moved on with my prepared questioning, desperately trying to salvage something, thinking less of myself each moment, my mind alternating between the thoughts *There must be some way to still be right* and *You don't know what you're talking about*.

"Oh, I love that movie!" an interviewee with a goatee said. "Classic film. Oh, wait, I'm thinking of *Fargo*. *Rushmore* is the one with Nic Cage?"

"I don't know," I said. I wrote *NIC CAGE* onto an otherwise blank page.

I began to try to play it off like I was interested in hearing about more than just *Rushmore*. I wanted my interview subjects to feel useful so they wouldn't get mad at me. I was wasting my time and theirs.

"Is that an actor you like?" I said, my pen ready to note his answer.

"Cage? Yeah, I guess so."

Part of me started to hope I would not be able to find someone who had seen *Rushmore*, so my project, already doomed by its dumbass premise, would have reasons outside my dumbass sensibilities for failing, but Catie, my fifth and final interviewee, had seen it.

"Not recently," she said. "But yeah, of course. It's great."

She had given me a headshot at the start of our interview, before we sat down in chairs I had positioned facing each other in the middle of the room like I was conducting an interview for *60 Minutes*. Catie was smiling confidently in the photo, projecting the perfect arrangement of features of the Approachable and Somewhat Goofy Babe for which she was seeking parts. She had mistaken my Craigslist ad for some kind of performance opportunity, and, though I could see the misunderstanding in her emails to me, I did not correct her assumption.

Catie laughed at most things I said, appearing comfortable and genuine. She loved my *Rushmore* idea, she said she found it hilarious, and wanted to be part of the project in any way she could. She said she loved that I was doing something experimental, approved of my Craigslist approach, wanted to know more about my body of work. I told her I was mostly a painter but was starting to get into film work.

"That's honestly amazing," she said, her eyes wide and bright. She touched my arm in a way that I knew was calculated to make me feel close with her. Still, it worked. I wanted her to follow me around my life validating me.

"There's so much pressure to limit yourself to one mode of expression. And why? Why not follow your heart? You only get one lifetime."

"It's crazy that Bill Murray is such a cult figure," she said, pulling her long blond bangs over her left eyebrow in a way that looked practiced. "I mean, I love him. But I can never figure out what it is about him that gives him this enduring appeal with so many people."

Maybe Catie's opinions about Bill Murray could be woven into my remake. I could give his character more screen time than was warranted by the script. (It didn't occur to me until this moment that I'd probably have to write a script.) Catie herself, and her overestimation of her role in this project, could also be part of the film. Maybe I could have Catie narrate, for example. I had already recorded her describing the movie. I could cut it up and use that. Maybe this wouldn't be so bad.

I listened to Catie describe *Rushmore* in as much detail as she could remember, taking notes while my camera recorded her. The way she told it, the story in *Rushmore* didn't quite make sense. But that was a good thing. No need to have a reliable source of information when the whole point was to adapt the movie based on peoples' foggy memories. All this was good. Great. This was going to work.

"Can I buy you a beer?" I asked when we were done. But Catie had to go in for a shift at Banana Republic.

"Let me know if you need anything else," she said. "Again, I'd love to help in any way I can. And make sure to tell me when it gets accepted to South By." (I may have implied I was going to submit the finished project to film festivals.)

Hello! I'm Joey, and I'm compensating for my fear of engaging with the world by creating work that attempts to force me to engage with the world about something I don't know anything about or care about, chosen at random.

I point to my own face on a large projection screen.

Which allows me to create self-reflexive work with a built-in shield of contemporary film criticism and social engagement.

Someone in the audience: Why does your subject look so depressed?

Which serves to limit how much others can talk about me as a person when they talk about my work.

Me, grinning suspiciously: What is a subject but a window to the soul (whatever that means)?

Which is probably indicative of how little I'm willing to change my shitty personality. Or how much I can project my shitty personality onto Jason Schwartzman or Bill Murray.

Me: Look, this is all to say that Rushmore *is a consumer product . . .*

Or steer the conversation to some trite art student topic like whether or not Wes Anderson's work is art or commodity.

I turn on the DVD player to show my Rushmore *remake.*

And whether that view changes when seen through another layer of artistic representation (mine). Probably not, but whatever.

30% of an artist's life is devoted to pretending you like your own ideas

10% is finding enjoyment in making huge irreparable mistakes

6% is going along with other people's interpretations of your art

5% is believing your own bullshit, even as you're in the process of making it up

10% is trying to view your art from your current love interest's perspective

9% is keeping a journal by your bed

5% is remembering the feeling of being loudly dissed by the person you most idolized in third grade

5% is finding something obscure to reference constantly

20% is ignoring the people who like your work

"Do you think you could ever fuck someone without developing feelings?" Suz said. We were hanging out in her painting studio while Suz worked on a large painting of what looked like the back of a woman's head. I was supposed to be typing out answers to my Art History prompts, but instead I had connected to Wi-Fi and started reading an article titled *"Pretty Little Liars*—What Happened to Alison."

"It sounds fun to try," I said.

"I just always get emotionally invested and, like, I have so much going on and all these goals and plans and then some guy comes along and I'm like, *Want to watch movies in your unmade bed until five p.m.?*"

"That sounds really cute."

"Ah, you're not helping."

"I guess I don't see what's wrong with enjoying your life."

Suz got quiet and I felt unsure if I had said something to upset her. I was probably missing the point or focusing on the wrong information.

"Anyway, I fucked Freddie from our Intro to Sculpture class," she said.

I dramatically fell back into my chair and covered my mouth with my hands. Suz reached over to slap me gently on the shoulder and then dipped a brush in neon orange paint and swept it elegantly across the canvas in a way I would never have expected.

"Shut up," she said, laughing. "And can I tell you something gross? He held me after, and I wanted to stay there forever."

Once Freddie had brought these small disintegrating vessels into Intro to Sculpture. He had made them out of small saliva-moistened bits of chewed-up wood fiber. I thought they were okay. But Freddie sulked out of class right after his critique because everyone was suggesting using glue instead of saliva. I could understand his reaction. It's hard to bring work to class, present it as representative of your very soul, then have it be suggested that you may not have thought everything through. It feels like being told you don't know who you are, or that you need to change the essence of your being. Although in some cases, I don't know, maybe you do need to change. I mean, you're chewing pieces of wood.

I gave her a pained look.

"I know," she said. "I know."

I met up again with Suz at the student lounge at 9:30 a.m. the next day. We both had classes that started at 10:00, and she wanted to show me some thumbnails for a "digital landscape" she was planning to start, whatever that meant. We sat on hard couches and watched rain fall in the parking lot outside.

The thumbnails themselves were large, taking up the full nine-by-twelve-inch page of her sketchbook, made with colored pencil or oil pastel and scraps of textured fabric and cutout pieces of blurry photographs. They were fun to look at. I would have considered them finished artworks.

"I really like these," I said.

"Where the pink leather is would be like a pulsing light that takes over the entire screen every forty-five seconds. Kind of like if a heartbeat was a visual sensation."

I thought about this, looking at the scrap of pink leather taped to the side of one of the drawings. I would never have thought of using leather as a shorthand for pulsing light. My mind was prone to the obvious, so set on interpreting things in a literal way rather than experiencing life and color and universal vibrations the way Suz did, letting ideas move and consume and disorient her, letting them come out in ways that might not be decipherable to anyone without her explanation.

"That's awesome," I said, handing her sketchbook back to her.

Suz started reading from a book and I flipped through my sketches from the last few days. After a while, Suz got up and left, then came back with two coffee cups, handing one to me.

"I was thinking I'll just use Catie's memory of *Rushmore* and no one else's," I said. "I don't want to go through the whole Craigslist thing again to find more people."

"Hmm," Suz said, stirring cream into her coffee.

"Do you think that's a good idea?" I said.

I hoped it was obvious that I meant it was a good idea *given the context of the desperation of my situation,* and not a good idea in general. Obviously this was the stupidest idea of my life.

"So instead of remaking the film from the collective memory, you'd remake just one person's idea of it?"

"Yeah," I said, impressed by how "the collective memory" sounded, saddened that the phrase was now something I could not use to describe my project.

"That could work. But why Catie? Because she was the first person you found who saw the movie?"

Suz stared into her coffee mug sleepily. I could tell she was thinking about her own art again.

I thought of Jenny, sitting on the floor against our coffee table sometime after she stopped going to high school. Looking down at a Cup O' Noodles in her lap, waiting for the noodles to soften, slowly nodding off.

"Jenny!" I had screamed. She fell over sideways, spilling hot Cup O' Noodles all over her chest and legs, still not waking up.

"Yeah. Because she was the first person," I said, knowing how lazy that sounded. "But there would always be a limited scope to the project anyway. Even my original idea would have been whoever happened to respond to my Craigslist post. I would never have had the scope to get an actual cultural collective interpretation. That would take resources I'll never have."

"My advice, and, okay, I know this is going to sound really, like, woo-woo, and I apologize," Suz said. "My advice is to let the project have its own inner life. Let it develop in its own way. You can't control it any more than you can control anything."

I understood the words but not how I could apply them to something I had to make. Understanding I was still struggling with the concept, she said, "Think of it as though you're trying to understand it, rather than invent it."

It was tempting to blame myself for my bad ideas. But maybe I could blame my Drawing I professor, who had stressed the idea of negative space in what I could see in retrospect was an overbearing way. Maybe I could blame the many drawings I had made for class since, trying to capture what I normally would have thought of as "not there" or "nothing." Maybe that process had stuck with me and was causing me to feel, ultimately, like it was the movies I had not seen that somehow made up the meaningful or interesting parts of my life. That the shape of all those unwatched movies, and *Rushmore* in particular, wasn't ever "not there," that it was, since its release, always in my subconscious, and influencing things in my world without my knowing, giving shape to what I thought was real.

I texted Catie, *Were you w anyone when you saw Rushmore the first time? Do you remember what else you did that day? Or anything? Did you talk about the movie w anyone after?*

I was worried that Catie had rewatched *Rushmore* since we last spoke, which would taint her memories of the film. But I also didn't care. Working with other people on a project diminished the amount of control I had. Which was fine. Good.

How do we know Max is in love w his teacher? I texted. *Is it voice over or does he tell somebody or . . .*

Ok, so . . . Catie texted within minutes, followed by several paragraphs of her memories surrounding her own life when she first saw *Rushmore*, how she connected to Max because of his tendency to overachieve and underachieve at the same time, correcting me on the fact that Max wasn't in love with his teacher but rather *a* teacher, none of it all that helpful to me.

The front of my phone lit up with my mom's name and phone number. We hadn't talked since a few days before when I refused to quit college to watch my nephew while my sister screwed someone from GameStop.

"Can you call Jenny and ask her to stop being such a selfish bitch? She needs to come home."

"How exactly am I supposed to phrase that?" I said.

"I don't know, Joey. But if things continue like they are, I'm going to pack my things and no one is going to hear from me ever again."

She'd made me promise to call Jenny, but I knew I wouldn't. Being a selfish bitch was such a personal choice, and it didn't feel right to suggest how or when a person should or shouldn't do it. Plus, I didn't believe there was ever an example of someone asking someone to stop being a bitch and it working.

I pressed the buttons on my phone that would bring up Jenny's number, trying to imagine what it would feel like if Mom had really run away, what I might say to Jenny about it.

Then I imagined what would happen if I disappeared, how long it would take my family to realize I was gone, if they would ever go looking for me.

I talked Suz into posing for me for an hour. I needed drawings to fill up my daily sketchbook for Drawing II class, which I had been neglecting for over a week. It was a habit of mine to fill up sketchbook pages in a panic the night before they were due. It was so easy to neglect the art assignments I cared about most in favor of the ones that made me doubt everything I knew about myself.

Suz put on a floral bikini bottom and lounged on my hardwood floor. *I Love Lucy* played on her laptop nearby. Suz laughed out loud at Lucy and I had to remind her to hold still. I took the shade off my standing lamp and rested the pole against a chair behind her, creating dramatic lighting.

Suz was fun to draw. I had drawn her so many times the details came as naturally to me as the lines of my own face. I drew the sharp turn of her jaw almost from memory, the way it led all the way up to the tops of her ears in a single line, cheekbones that caught the light at a three-quarter angle, always a clump of dark curly black hair crossing her forehead to create the only bit of texture against her poreless skin, and nostrils that were slightly visible straight on, a detail that I found trustworthy and emotionally relatable (though I couldn't explain what this meant).

"I love that we're supposed to believe Lucy thinks Ricky is going to kill her because she got freaked out from reading a scary novel," Suz said.

"Oh my god, I know. Like, she's supposed to be this smart and scheming character but also doesn't have a brain?"

"What a goddamn American hero."

Suz moved to scratch her foot and a chunk of hair fell into her face where it wasn't before, blocking everything but a sliver of profile at an odd angle. I used the side of my pencil to make thick strokes for the hair, leaving nothing showing but two small lumps of lips, a small lump of nose, the flickering ends of her eyelashes.

We walked to Corner Liquor, got some tall cans to stuff into Suz's backpack, and then walked to a party at Suz's friend Orin's apartment. As we walked off the busy main road into the residential streets, Suz told me about a film she had watched the night before called *The God of Cookery*. Something about someone rudely criticizing chefs as a job and later mass-producing canned meatballs as revenge.

"You should just watch it. I'll give you the DVD and you can return it to the library for me," she said.

"Okay, sweet," I said, fairly sure I wouldn't watch it.

The "apartment" was a house. I couldn't remember if Suz had said the word *apartment* or if I had assumed that all college students lived in apartments, not stand-alone properties in one of the most expensive cities in the world. The door was ajar and we heard people talking, so we walked into the house without knocking. There were thirty or forty people in the entry room, which I understood to be a living room based on the one piece of furniture it held: a sad white IKEA couch. A few were sitting on the ground looking at cards scattered across the floor, but most were standing, holding beer bottles or wineglasses, talking animatedly, showing each other things on their phones. I left Suz to find a toilet.

There was what appeared to be original wood crown molding throughout the house, not sloppily painted over a hundred times like the molding in my apartment. I found the long line outside the bathroom, and I wished I had gotten my beer from Suz's backpack so I could drink it while I waited. It was strange to be unaccompanied in a stranger's home completely sober. I bit my fingernails, moved six inches closer to the bathroom after two people exited together, and then started biting a cuticle. Someone a few places in front of me in line lit a joint. I turned around to look behind me to see if I could spot Suz, ask her to bring me my beer through psychic communication, but instead I made eye contact with the girl standing behind me, who I recognized from my 3D Materials class two semesters ago. Lydia something. Graphic Design, maybe.

"Oh, hi," I said, happy to recognize someone.

"Hey," Lydia said. She took her phone out of her back pocket and started typing on it. I waited a few seconds to see if she would look back up from her phone, but she did not. She had the same hairstyle as Karen O from the "Maps" video. When I turned around, a joint was being handed to me.

"Oh my," I said. I took the joint between my thumb and index finger with so much delicacy it must have looked like fear, reminding myself of some old woman who spent her whole fucking life being careful and now, in her late nineties, was trying to figure out what she had missed out on all those years ago outside the soda fountain. I inhaled weakly.

I handed the joint back to the guy who handed it to me, and he indicated I should send it the other way.

"What good manners, young man," I said, continuing the joke about me being an old woman for an audience of only myself.

I handed the joint to Lydia, who took it from me without looking. Then I shuffled six inches forward as someone else exited the bathroom.

I wandered around until I heard Suz in the distance yelling passionately, "Radiohead sucks."

"Radiohead is fine," another voice said.

"They're so bad, though."

I walked toward the voices with my eyes mostly closed. I had smoked too much, but it also felt like I had not smoked anything. Every few seconds I remembered who I was like a crushing weight over my body. I wanted to not remember, just for a little while. Maybe not remembering who I was for a little while would help me to change into someone less mortifying.

"It's okay though."

"It's okay to be bad?"

"Radiohead has every right to be bad."

"So you admit they're bad?"

I followed Suz's voice until I found her and saw that the second voice was Freddie's.

"No, I'm just admitting they're Radiohead," he said, smiling big and squinting his eyes. He was doing a James Franco impression, I realized. Or, he thought he was as hot as James Franco and that a squinty smile would be interpreted as seductive. But even James Franco couldn't always pull that off. I remembered watching *Eat Pray Love* and thinking, *James Franco thinks that's his thing. He thinks that's his thing so much that it doesn't even work like it's supposed to. All I can think when he does it is* James Franco is doing that thing again.

Suz smiled shyly and sucked down the rest of her beer. I approached them slowly, trying to remember any thought in the world.

"Has anyone ever tried to remember what they were just thinking about?" I said.

Suz made eye contact with me in a way that conveyed approval at the level of my drug-induced disorientation, annoyance that I was interrupting her conversation with Freddie, and a patronizing patience that made me sad for myself.

"You just said the most high thing someone can say," Freddie said, turning his body slightly away from mine so as to subtly exclude me.

"Did you guys ever read Robert Frost?" I said (my big attempt at holding everyone's attention with my top-shelf conversation skills).

"I think so," Suz said.

"In third grade my class had to take turns reciting poems and for some reason I always pretended I had memorized the poem that had been assigned to me for some other reason not pertaining to the assignment. I'd be like, *Who, me? A Robert Frost poem? Oh okay, sure, I think I can remember one or two off the top of my head.*"

"That's so funny," Suz said, but she didn't laugh.

My middle school had shared a courtyard with the high school, and once during seventh grade an older guy I didn't know sat down next to me at the picnic table. He was sort of hot in a dirt-bag way.

"Cool drawing," he said, gesturing to my open sketchbook. Then, pointing to my shirt, "Is that Chewbacca? Dude, awesome."

I started going off about whatever *Star Wars* novel I was reading at the time, excited that a guy was interested in my opinions on this, imagining what my friend Lindsay would think when I inevitably started dating this filthy older teenager.

Lindsay would say: *Is that your boyfriend?*

I would say: *Yes.*

Lindsay would say: *He's hot.*

Me, pretending to know what "giving head" meant and also that I'd know how to qualify it: *He gives great head.*

Lindsay would say: *What's so great about it?*

Me, not wanting to say too much in case I'm working with the wrong definition of "head": *I don't kiss and tell!*

But then the guy pressed a baggie into my hand and, in a deeper, menacing voice, said, "This is for your sister. If she doesn't get it, I will personally kick your ass."

"Is this drugs?"

He said, "Put it in your fucking bag and run along, freak."

I packed up my things and ran along indeed, to the girls' bathroom to hyperventilate.

When I was fifteen, I had sex with my neighbor Keaton at a house party out by Mervyn's. I felt that never having done it held me back intellectually. I had to know what it was. The risk factor of doing it intrigued me. Maybe I was into risky behavior. There were other risky things I did that I found to be worth the risk. Wetting a dirty paintbrush with my tongue, for example. Eating school lunch. Getting into a car with my mother.

Once I had had sex, it was easier to focus on other things. I was doing these close-up portraits of myself and people I knew using black fine-point Sharpies I kept stealing from my P.E. teacher's desk.

Lindsay didn't believe me when I told her I had done it. She was the one who boys liked. She was the risk-taker. She was the one who did things first. It called into question the delicate balance of inequality our friendship was founded on.

"Okay. Don't believe me," I said. My nonchalance about the subject finally convinced her.

Something changed in Lindsay after that. She was more interested in spending time with me, called me more, wanted me to come over for sleepovers, but was also meaner to me when we were together. She called our classmates in front of me and told them I was in love with them, or talking shit, or wanted to fight.

I think she wanted me to protest, but instead I would get out my sketchbook and make drawings of our interactions. I made cartoony representations of the two of us in her room, her sitting in front of her computer making playlists and chatting on AIM, me on her bed looking through her makeup box. I put the mean things she said to me in boxes below the drawings.

"I can't believe you think that's what my nose looks like," she said.

I made friends with Lindsay when we were five. She told me how to play with plastic vegetables and plastic cooking utensils.

I was attached to her and afraid of everyone else to such a degree that our teacher recommended we be placed in the same first-grade class. Mrs. Abbott thought our separation would be unbearable for me.

As we grew up we were always "Lindsay and Joey," as a single unit, e.g., "Lindsay and Joey started wearing matching gray hoodies and claiming they're in a gang," "Lindsay and Joey have befriended the janitor," "Lindsay and Joey are hitchhiking across town to hang out with a twenty-nine-year-old man named Justin because he promised to buy them Natty Ice."

I often wished her family would move away. I wondered who I would be if half my personality wasn't defined by another person's actions. Who would I hang out with if someone else wasn't deciding for me? What might I find out about myself? But I wasn't strong enough to tear myself away from her.

"Can I tell you something?" Jenny said.

"Sure," I said. It was the day before Jenny's due date, and we had walked to Burger King for a buttload of value-menu items, my treat. We had to wait a long time for our food, and when it finally came, they had given us extra fries and extra nuggets. We were eating like royalty. It was fun to pig out with a pregnant girl. People looked at us with bemusement and approval, thinking Jenny was fulfilling a goofy craving. An old man carried an unwrapped Whopper over to us and said "Cheers" and we all touched burgers.

"I tried heroin," she said.

"What? Recently?" My mouth was full of onion rings but I stopped chewing.

"Just to see what it was like. I kept hearing people talk about it. I wanted to know what the big deal was."

I took a big gulp of Sprite to clear my mouth and said, "While you were pregnant?"

"Fuck you," she said. "You're just like Mom. You can't wait until someone fucks up." She threw the rest of the food in a bag, including the onion rings I was still eating, then stood up, pulling her tank top down over her large stomach.

"You can't wait to point it out when they do. You think you're a good person. Well, you aren't. You're fucking cold and shitty."

She walked out the door and to the left, toward the back of the Burger King where there were no windows for me to see which direction she was going. And suddenly I was sitting at a table alone with some dirty napkins and used ketchup packets.

what we don't yet
understand about
family is <u>WHY</u>
it continues after
it stops benefiting
anyone.

If my life were a screenplay, at some point my character would have to realize she wasn't the lead role. She was a supporting actor for other characters to project things onto, blame, harbor insecurities about, or altogether ignore.

My character description would say, "short brunette who compensates for her plain looks with a nose piercing and a bunch of large, ornate rings," and my character, not knowing whether "short" referred to her hair or body, and not wanting to bother anyone by asking, would simply be short in both hair and stature.

Her biggest scene would be one in which she holds her drunk sister's hair back while she barfs and cries, giving an uplifting lecture about how everything is going to be okay because lots of people get drunk before they know they are pregnant and everything turns out fine, so what could be so wrong with getting drunk when you do know? The knowing couldn't possibly make it worse. This is a scene she can't pull off because it is supposed to come across as patient and loving and accepting of her sister's unfortunate circumstances, but she physically can't stop making judgmental faces and sighing with impatience, which makes the audience wonder why she is there at all, and what she is adding to the scene that couldn't be accomplished by a hair clip.

The screenplay follows my character around after that, but the audience continues thinking about the sister. What happened with her baby? Will she ever get her life together? How did she get herself into this mess in the first place? The audience doesn't get to know, because my character doesn't feel the same impulse to understand her sister that others do, but the audience does ultimately find out the difference between Conté crayons and pastels.

"This is important to me and I want you to care," my character would say, breaking the fourth wall.

"Yes! We do! Totally!" the audience would say, checking their phones.

catdog theme song lyrics| 🔍

rushmore cliffsnotes no spoilers   history
pop tart nutritional value   history
how long can I live just on poptarts   history
what flavor pop tart is most healthy   history
lee krasner   history
was monet a bitch   history
why so many angry dreams   history

close

Diana walked up to the wooden box I was sitting on in the main hall on campus, looking at a babysitting website on my laptop.

"I love that sweater," Diana said. I looked down to remember what sweater I was wearing, even though there was only one sweater it could have been. It was a slouchy red knit pullover with black circles on the front that I always wore, the only sweater I owned. "I think you were wearing it the last time I saw you, and I was like, *damn, I like that sweater*, but I never said it."

I wished I had a new sweater for every time someone told me I was wearing this sweater the last time they saw me.

"Thanks, I got it at a vintage store Suz took me to in the Tenderloin."

"Oh, I know that one," Diana said. "It's bomb."

"I'm, uh, taking a quiz about what kind of shower caddy I am," I said, not sure why I was offering up a lie for no reason, especially one that made me seem stupid, but hoped it would make her lose interest in me and go do something else. Diana was Suz's roommate, a plain girl who was nonetheless outgoing and confident. She didn't have any discernible style, which rattled me. Most people at our school made loud, overstated fashion choices that helped you understand who they were without talking to them. Diana wore blue jeans, striped shirts from the Gap, no makeup, her honey-blond hair always tied in a low ponytail, comfortable projecting the fact that her personality was boring, boring, boring. She reminded me of the girls who passed for popular at my high school, not because they were particularly well liked but because they seemed confident their own existence mattered.

Can't relate, unfortunately.

She sat down next to me, pulled out *The Rings of Saturn* by W. G. Sebald, and set it beside her. She stared ahead peacefully, like sitting together was a relaxing activity worth savoring. We sat together in silence for a few minutes, then she picked her book back up.

"Have you read this?" she said.

"Mm, no," I said.

"I hate it," she said.

"Oh, don't read it then?"

"I have to for a class."

She turned the book around to show me a page with notes written all over it in several different ink colors. There were more handwritten notes than typed text.

"This is me trying to understand what the fuck is going on on page three."

"Damn," I said. "That looks painful."

I angled my computer screen so Diana would have no way to see it, and tried to finish filling out a questionnaire about my babysitting qualifications, which mostly consisted of my experience troubleshooting Brian's shitty babyhood with my mom over the phone from a hundred miles away. I had watched him a lot before I moved to college, but he was so tiny then, and mostly slept.

I specialize in newborn care, I wrote.

Diana said, "Oh my god, what?" to herself while looking at her phone, then laughed loudly and unselfconsciously, as if she were in a room full of people laughing. She moved easily through the world, clearly under the assumption that all people would like her by default. It was charming, kind of, and a healthy perspective, probably. But I was sick of reminders that there were other ways to be, and that I could be improving myself as a person.

I went back to my questionnaire. *Are you CPR certified?* I selected "no" and then submitted the form without finishing it. No one was going to hire my non-CPR-certified ass.

"My mom just sent me this video of her and my dad singing that 'Fuck You' song," she said. She turned her phone screen to me, and I could see two well-dressed old people dancing stupidly.

I laughed in a socially appropriate manner, not wanting to encourage the conversation but not wanting to be unfriendly either, wanting mostly to continue my pointless job search that would never, I knew in my heart, end in employment. "I don't even know what that is," I said.

"That CeeLo song."

I looked at her blankly, waiting for more information.

"You know it, for sure. Anyway, they're always sending me random videos of themselves. I think they're lonely. Sometimes I feel like I don't give them enough of my attention."

"Oh really? Weird," I said, still not sure what reaction I was supposed to be having. Did she find herself so interesting that someone she barely knew would want to be bombarded with information about her homework and her family? I longed to be the kind of person who could open up so naturally and effortlessly, but when I was confronted with such a person, it made me feel both inadequate and put-upon. She seemed to sense my hostility and stopped talking to me. She read quietly from her book until I closed my laptop a few minutes later and, nodding my head as a goodbye, headed over to Art and Madness.

Allen, appearing from nowhere in the middle of the school court-yard, walked right up to me even though I was avoiding eye contact.

"Joey! Did you know about our new pantry program?"

Allen was a tall, dark-haired man with thin wire glasses seemingly employed by the school to get people more involved in extracurricular activities. I had met him when I put my name on the job board list at the beginning of sophomore year, and he eagerly addressed me by name every time he saw me since that day. He was Egyptian, which I knew because one time I had asked him, "What are you?" (meaning, like, what was his job title) and he said, "Egyptian," and I was embarrassed he thought I would ask a question like that, especially in the somewhat rude tone of voice I had taken, so I said, "Amazum" ("awesome" and "amazing" accidentally jumbled into one word) and then stood there with my mouth open and he said, "What are you?" and I said, "Nothing."

"No," I said, with no hint of interest.

"You should check it out! It's in the last room on the right in the Student Center. There are free snacks and nonperishable goods for the students. It's amazing and underutilized. I want everyone to know about it."

"Oh, okay," I said.

Allen was a nice guy. I had nothing against Allen. I could tell he was trying to help. But I always felt an urgent need to get away from him.

"You can also donate items or money to the program," Allen said as I walked past him.

I did go to the Student Center, and to the last room on the right, which was more of a closet than a room. Protein bars, jars of peanut butter, pita chips, Cup O' Noodles, canned fruit, canned raviolis, and room-temperature sodas in weird flavors lined a few wire shelves.

There was a large sign on the wall that read ALL ITEMS ARE FREE. PLEASE TAKE ONLY WHAT YOU WILL USE. DON'T LEAVE ITEMS. TO DONATE ITEMS GO TO STUDENT CENTER OFFICE. THANK YOU.

I stuffed menstrual pads and peanut butter into my backpack and turned to leave, then turned back into the room and grabbed a couple each of protein bars, canned raviolis, and Cup O' Noodles.

I arrived at Suz's apartment building and rang the buzzer. There were two entrances, and one of the first times I came over, at 9:00 p.m., I pushed the left buzzer instead of the right buzzer and an old man answered the wrong door and yelled at me for waking him up. I felt very bad, and ever since then, even though I was confident that she lived in the right-hand unit, I peeked into the glass of the door to see Suz's blue vintage road bike propped up in the entryway before I buzzed.

"I have procured all junk foods ever made," Suz said as she opened the door. "Get ready for a wild night."

She led me into the kitchen and showed me an enormous stack of various junk foods: organic corn chips, sour candy straws, organic white cheddar popcorn, ranch Pringles, two boxes of Amy's pizza rolls, and Zevia cream soda. She looked at me intensely and emptied both boxes of pizza rolls onto a baking tray while maintaining dramatic eye contact.

I made a concerned but playful expression, pretending I was an old woman, like, *Oh, dear me*. It was a good amount of pizza rolls, but by no means an impossible amount.

"I'll try," I said, knowing I could and would do it, that I could, indeed, eat all the pizza rolls by myself, even if I wasn't particularly hungry. In fact, I was already thinking that I would have to force myself to eat the pizza rolls at a slower rate than I would normally so that Suz could retain her false belief that this was a lot of pizza rolls.

"I'm always in a weird mood after showing work. I like to drown myself in salt and oil."

I opened my backpack to reveal my own contribution to the night: a fifth of Jack Daniel's and two cans of ginger ale I had gotten from the Student Center pantry. I took two ceramic mugs from her cabinet, handmade by a friend of her mother's, and poured the liquids into them carefully.

"Do you have any vine charcoal I can borrow?" I said.

"I do." She gestured to her stack of art boxes next to her dining table, an invitation.

I mixed us both drinks, set hers on the counter next to the stove, and took mine over to her art boxes.

"Check that teal box first. I think it's in there."

I found some charcoal in a fancy pencil case in the teal art box and took out my sketchbook to do some two-minute life drawings (an assignment for Drawing II) of Suz standing in her kitchen.

"Are you in any classes with Herta Meyer?" I said.

"Oh, that tall, muscular blond chick?" Suz said.

"Yeah."

"I was in Drawing I with her first semester last year. She drew a pile of bones once for a still life assignment and everyone was like, *Uh, where'd you get a pile of bones?*"

"I wish I were her friend. She wrote this insane story for our English class. She's one of the weirdest people at school I think. And she always says these intense cryptic things, like, 'A secret is a story not worth telling.'"

"Huh," said Suz.

I did quick sketches of her standing in front of the oven as she arranged the pizza rolls in neat rows on the tray, waiting for the oven to preheat. I wondered if I had sounded too enthusiastic about Herta, if it had sounded like I was in search of new friends because I was tired of my current options.

"They should make ranch soda," I said after three ginger whiskeys. I had just drunk the crumbs from the end of the Pringles can and felt inspired.

"I think I saw that in Germany," Suz said.

"When did you go to Germany?"

"I went after high school graduation with a few friends from my class. It was a gift from my parents. I mostly just got wasted and went to museums."

On my thirteenth birthday my mom had handed me a velvet jewelry box, a gift. I opened it and saw a delicate gold bracelet, the same one I had seen in her jewelry box for as long as I could remember. An heirloom. I was touched. Mom then kissed me on the mouth and I smelled her vodka breath. She lay on the couch and attempted to hand me the remote control but couldn't hold her arm up. "Birthday television," she slurred. I turned on Nickelodeon, and when she fell asleep a few minutes later, I put the bracelet back in her jewelry box, not wanting to be accused of theft. The proximity I now had to a frivolous teenage trip to Germany embarrassed me so much my face turned red. It felt as if I had invented the idea of international teen travel just to piss off my family. I pulled out my phone to atone.

Hows it going? I texted my mom. I dropped a pizza roll into my mouth.

My phone vibrated and, seeing it was my mom, I pressed the button to make the noise stop.

"I'm having a sudden nostalgia for 'Kissed by a Rose'–era Seal," Suz said.

"Is there any other Seal?" I said.

My mom called again as soon as my phone showed that the previous call was missed. Couldn't I just send a text without it turning into a thing? But then I imagined her sprawled on the side of the road somewhere in a hit-and-run that almost broke her phone but not quite fully—it is still able to call me and, somehow, only me.

"Hello?" I said.

"Did you ever talk to Jenny after I told you to call her?"

"No," I said. "I'm kind of busy. What's up?"

"Well, have you heard from her at all? She's missing."

"She's missing? In what way?"

I stood up and made a gesture to Suz like, *one minute, this is nothing*, and left her bedroom to stand at the farthest point of her hallway, near the front door.

"She hasn't been home since the police thing last week and I finally got ahold of Katie and she said Jenny left a few nights ago saying she was going over to some guy's house who owed her money and she never came back. I have to go to work in five hours and I don't know what to do with him. I can't stay home with a baby and I have no idea where she is and she isn't answering her phone. I'm going to lose my job."

"Shit. Can Alicia watch him?"

"She's in Vegas on her honeymoon," she said, sounding angry with me for making such an unhelpful suggestion. Or maybe she was angry with Alicia for having a honeymoon.

"Okay, sorry. Maybe that neighbor lady again?"

"I have to go," she said, sounding even more pissed. "Please pray for Jenny to come back by this weekend. I have a nail appointment."

"Okay."

She hung up but I said, "Bye," into a dead line anyway in case Suz was listening.

"Who is missing?" Suz said.

I considered the two paths that diverged in front of me. The first path was one where Suz continued to believe that my upbringing was only mildly, playfully trashy, something that you'd see in a movie about how fun it could be to be poor, one in which I used Scotch tape to make a line on the floor to divide my side of the room from my sister's and our mom cries, *weeps*, at the Scotch tape money I wasted.

The second path was the one where I told Suz my sister was a crackhead, that I hadn't tried to help her, that nobody really had, that nobody really even thought about helping, that our mom was too busy dating and drinking to bother with anything other than keeping her job, which was, in itself, a miraculous achievement, a job that fed my entire family, and also that I had abandoned my family not in search of answers or help, but to understand myself through art, that Suz herself was an actor in this trashy play, and by being present and funny and cool in every way I found important, she made me feel like I had gained entry to something exclusive, she was guiding me away from my home, making me believe that *home* was a synonym for *past* and that a "friend" could be someone I actually enjoyed talking to.

Telling her about my sister would invite her to have private thoughts about my morality, or about the costs a friendship with me could incur, or change her valuation of me as a person. Knowing I chose not to help my own sister in her most helpless moments would paint me as an untrustworthy person. I wanted Suz to trust me, and count on me, and believe that I would help her if she needed me. And? I wanted her to need me. I wanted to fulfill that need. Maybe I wouldn't fulfill the need. Maybe I would, in the moment, turn my back to her, just like I do to my crackhead sister whenever the opportunity presents itself. Maybe I am indeed evil and want to see others fail as a way to see myself as ever so slightly better. But I would never know unless someone else needed me someday.

Not telling her was the truth, too, in a way. Things can be true without going into great detail about them. Things can be shrouded in mystery. Some people like mystery.

"Nobody," I said. "Just some fun family drama."

I adjusted my face to remove whatever worry or panic might've been on it, and looked down at my hands.

I always look down at my hands when I feel like I've betrayed someone.

"Oh okay. It sounded serious."

"No. My sister is kind of a party animal. My mom always freaks out when she isn't home in time for dinner."

I opened my sketchbook and showed her the drawings I had done of her earlier in the night, flipping through the pages and looking up to see her reaction.

"I love these," she said, scooting closer to me on the floor. "You really captured the movement." She pointed to one in which she is bending over to put a pan of pizza rolls into the oven.

I was the last person to get to Drawing II on Thursday, which was always Crit Day, so I had to hang my drawings up in the far corner, by the entrance. The corner was not a great place to hang drawings for crit, because the light was dim there and because your crit would be last, and everyone would be worn out from critiquing work by that point and not have much to say.

This week, our assignment was "Charcoal." I had three drawings, which I hurriedly taped up side by side with blue painter's tape.

[IMG 1] [Charcoal self-portrait.]

[IMG 2] [Charcoal self-portrait in which I'm drawing a self-portrait in charcoal.]

[IMG 3] [Another charcoal self-portrait drawn using the first self-portrait as reference.]

I sat down at a studio bench and pulled my sketchbook out so I could draw during everyone else's critique. Our professor was a prolific magazine illustrator with a whimsical style, and our work was usually praised only when we used dainty and irregular lines similar to his. My thick, smudgy lines felt like an intentional rebellion against his aesthetic.

Most of my classmates hung single images, shadowy figures in dramatic lighting, which was an easy choice for charcoal. Faces included an awkward amount of detail. People were comfortable letting a single line or two represent an entire torso, but they'd fill in faces with every eyelash and worry line they knew to be there, even if the lighting would have rendered it invisible.

I looked up from my sketchbook when it was finally my turn for critique.

"There is something disturbing about the intensity of the expression, juxtaposed with the act of the artist consciously watching herself. There is a playful energy to the continued replication of this original drawing. It reminds the viewer of more contemporary technologies, like Xerox machines. It feels like the artist is commenting on charcoal as an outdated medium while still benefitting from the emotional and unpredictable nature of charcoal."

I thought: *I shall pretend I know what he means by "intense expression" and also not take offense at the implication that my natural resting face is "intense" and focus on what I think is a compliment about my work seeming fake somehow.*

"Thanks," I said, raising my hand. "Those are mine."

Professor Long walked away from my drawings, apparently finished with my crit after about two sentences, and began to wrap up class. "Charcoal is such an emotional medium. Each and every drawing on the wall today conveys a strong emotion: pain, romance . . ."

I thought: *Why do strong emotions have more value in art than weak or complicated or mundane emotions?* I rarely felt things strongly, yet these rare feelings of intensity were, in my view, overrepresented in art. Why didn't people want to see art about feeling mildly annoyed with a friend? Or the boredom that comes from eating the same thing day after day? Or the brief inexplicable sadness you felt when you saw something cute, like a fluffy cat?

Professor Long said, "I want you to continue exploring emotion in your work. Over the weekend, I want you to do a few still lifes in your sketchbook. Choose your subjects and tools carefully and think about what emotions you are conveying with these drawings. I want to see at least three."

I liked what Long said about my use of charcoal. Like I was trying to get the charcoal to be something else entirely by using it as if it were. My *Rushmore* thing could be a comment on outdated mediums. Maybe by remaking it with super-limited resources and lo-fi technology, I will be bringing a level of sincerity that wasn't there in the original film.

Half-Life of a Drawing

My own initial reaction: [positive]

My artist's statement: [meandering]

Critical response from others: [nonexistent]

Upon reflection: [deep shame]

My English class was asked to write short stories based on the concept of deceit. I wrote a piece based on my sister's habit of tricking me and our mom into taking her to Walmart under the guise of wanting a soda that was available only at Walmart, but in reality to meet with her drug dealer (a situation that was obvious to me and my mom but that we pretended to be ignorant of for some reason).

"They sell Diet Coke at the liquor store up the street," the protagonist in my story says to their sister.

"I don't want Diet Coke," the sister character says.

"You only ever drink Diet Coke," the protagonist says.

We printed our stories and distributed them to the class to read and comment on over the weekend.

Of all my classmates, Herta had written the only story I was interested in. It was about an acupuncturist who no longer believed in the power of acupuncture, and had started supplementing her practice with Reiki, unbeknownst to her clients. The acupuncturist is tormented by the deceit she is inflicting on her patients, but she also wants to cure their ills and transfer positive healing energy to them, which she believes the power of Reiki can offer.

Herta had easily caught me in a lie on the first day of English class, when we played Two Truths and a Lie as a way of introducing ourselves. My strategy was to lie about a mundane thing people typically don't lie about. But of course it must be obvious that I do not drink coffee daily. I couldn't even, under the pressure of the game, name a type of coffee other than "coffee."

"You don't drink coffee daily," Herta said decisively. "That is the lie."

She was older than most other students and had strong shoulders. I had crushy feelings toward her and often made an effort to sit across the table from her in class. But friendship between us would never happen. She was too mature and intellectual to ever find anything of value in me. She carried old leather-bound books. She was from another country. She owned a business having to do with the internet and now that she was financially stable was getting an art degree for fun. I was still a teenager. I cut my own bangs. I was putting myself into lifelong debt to figure out if I thought art was useful or not and was leaning toward "not."

She had never been explicit in any of her class introductions about what she had done prior to enrolling in art school, but I got the feeling she already had a degree in something impressive and virtuous, and was now studying art because she realized, after several years in whatever field she was in, that she had no further use for the money her job provided her. She was in my Drawing II class as well, and often made large, muddy, portrait-based pieces that our classmates found indecipherable and that she refused to explain. That refusal was part of her charm. Everyone else was eager to pretend they knew what they were doing, to anticipate the criticism people would have and attempt to convince us that it was all intentional. That if we didn't understand their work, we were meant to be confused or, better yet, believe the symbolism went over our heads. It reminded me of precocious children who pretended to already know everything adults tried to tell them.

In Herta's story, the acupuncturist's secret is found out by one of her clients, who threatens to send the information in an email to the acupuncturist's client mailing list. The last page is a long monologue from the acupuncturist, trying to explain her actions to the blackmailer, unsure herself what her motivations truly are, unsure what her life is about, and ending with the dramatic admission that she had pretended to like chocolate for forty-one years.

"Awesome story. I loved it," I said to Herta after class was over and everyone was getting up to leave, having said nothing during her somewhat negative class critique.

"Oh, thanks," she said, pulling cigarettes out of her bag. "Do you have a lighter?"

"I don't smoke," I said apologetically. I scanned the empty surfaces of the classroom in search of a lighter.

She walked toward the exit with a cigarette in her mouth and looked back at me before she left the room. I opened my backpack and pretended to look for something.

After everyone had left the classroom, I stopped pretending to look through my backpack, took my phone out, zipped the bag up, and walked out. I opened my text messages to text Suz about how stupid critique was.

Allen was standing by the drinking fountain outside of the class, looking at his phone. Why was he always lurking?

"Oh, hey, Joey," he said, looking up.

"Hi," I said, and rushed around the corner before he could say anything else.

I saw a sign advertising a job at the art store while I was there buying pens, and found the online job listing when I got home. The store was less than a mile from my apartment and the job came with a 15 percent employee discount.

A personality quiz was required with the application. The quiz was less an act of honest self-analysis than a warped psychological guessing game about what this art store might want in an employee.

Do you get angry when there is a conflict? Do you become frustrated when given work beyond your expected duties?

I checked the boxes that indicated a "No" response for the first two questions, which seemed like obviously the correct answers. *No, I am pleased when there is a conflict,* I imagined saying in a job interview. *I look for conflicts wherever I go because conflicts give me life. I am also thrilled by the prospect of extra work outside my skills or training, especially if there is nothing in it for me other than the minimum wage I am getting for my expected duties.*

I took a break from the quiz and opened a new tab for Facebook. I had a friend request from Diana. I clicked "accept" and then scrolled her page. Her profile picture, and many of her other posted photos, included a shaggy brown-and-white border collie. "Me and Karma," many of them were captioned. I "liked" several of them. I didn't like dogs but I thought it might serve me to be friendly. Then I navigated back to my personality quiz.

Are you someone who takes responsibility for others' errors?

Should an entry-level art store clerk be expected to take responsibility for another employee's mistake? Or were they trying to ask me if I was a narc? Being a narc was probably a good thing in the eyes of an employer who would ask a potential hire if they were a narc. So then the correct response would be, "No," as in *No, I'd throw a coworker under the bus if they made a mistake.* Was that an unfriendly thing to admit? Maybe it would be better to respond "Yes," as in *Yes, I allow myself to be taken advantage of by picking up the slack when my coworkers aren't doing their jobs.*

I didn't know what my answer would be if I was being honest about myself. I didn't like the idea of taking responsibility for others' errors, but maybe I would be up for it in certain situations. Should people take responsibility for others' errors at work? Is that a desirable workplace trait? Should I move toward that vibe?

I imagined the employees I saw regularly when I shopped there, wondering if they took responsibility for each other's shit. They seemed like people who might get beers together after work, or be in secret sexual relationships with one another.

I checked "No," hoping it meant I self-identified as a narc, hoping the art supply store was in fact looking for a narc. I could be their little narc.

I spoke from prepared notes about how personality was shaped by culture, how a film can be a reference point for an entire generation without anyone recognizing it as such. My *Rushmore* project, which I explained I had not begun filming, would represent a societal understanding of *Rushmore*. Fictional characters influenced how we viewed the world, I posited, even if we never thought about those characters, even if we had never consumed the media they existed within. My butthole itched, but I kept my hands in front of my body.

Cox said, "It makes me wonder why you define yourself by the holes in your knowledge and experience."

"This isn't really about me. It's about a collective understanding of a film," I said. "The way society . . ."

Rashid interrupted me to say, "But then why did you choose something you haven't seen?"

"I didn't want it to be tainted by my own biases," I said. "I wanted to portray it exactly as someone else described it. My own thoughts and biases included only subconsciously."

I wouldn't have avoided itching my knee right now, if it were itchy. I'd bend over and scratch it. There would be no deep consideration about whether or not it was appropriate. The act of scratching the knee would feel amazing for less than a second, and then it would feel neither good nor bad, but I'd continue scratching a little longer anyway.

Rashid said, "I guess I'd just like to see more of you in the piece."

"Yeah, it's like she's going out of her way to not be a participant in her own art," someone else said. I didn't look up to see who.

Why have we all decided to pretend we don't have buttholes? Or pretend that buttholes are numb to the environmental influences the rest of our bodies endure?

Rashid said, "You want to hold a mirror to society, but you don't want to acknowledge the experience of being the person holding that mirror."

Cox said, "That's actually a really interesting interpretation."

I said, "What is the point of making anything, anyway, when every-thing that already exists is so pointless?"

"Save the drama for the theater," Suz said.

"Have you seen *Bridezillas*?" I said, as if suddenly I realized that's where I would find meaning.

I found some downloadable episodes for free on Megaupload and, with a microwaved corn dog in each hand (I reached for packages of frozen corn dogs at the end of a long day the way some people reached for gin and tonics), began to search for answers within the choppily edited, stupidly narrated TV show.

Answers:

1. Humanity is in crisis and my personal artistic endeavors mean nothing to anyone but myself so the point is to satisfy myself in any way I can before it's too late and I become a bridezilla and every-thing is lost.

2. I don't deserve anything I have and maybe nobody does and the idea of "deserving" is a distraction from any possible meaning.

3. Making art is my way of tricking myself into believing that reality is something I can shape. (What am I referring to here? What art am I making?)

"Bridezilla is peak nothingness," Suz said. "A bridezilla accepts the nothingness, welcomes it, angrily insists that the nothingness is, in fact, everything."

"What does the voice-over represent?" I said.

"The voice-over is God," she said.

"So there is both nothingness and God?"

"Well, God can't actually do anything to help anybody. The nothingness exists despite her intentions. God is just there to offer judgment."

Rushmore (2011 Joelle Berry remake)

Jason Schwartzman meets an older woman in line at Jimmy John's. They spend an intense three-day weekend together, including one long breakfast montage. On Monday as he is getting ready to leave to go to class (Astronomy) she reveals that she is from the future, and wants him to drive her to the suburbs (they're in Sacramento) later that day and break into her old house so she can visit her deceased cat (deceased in the future she's time-traveling from; the cat is alive in the present time in which the movie takes place) whom she desperately misses.

In class:

Jason Schwartzman, his beret on kinda weird (from all the sex): Is time travel possible?

Astronomy Professor Bill Murray: Let me put it this way: We don't have any evidence that time travel is possible. But for a long time we didn't know well-designed, cheaply made Scandinavian furniture was possible.

[The entire class laughs.]

Jason Schwartzman: Right. So, if someone told me they were from the future, and they time-traveled here to have sex with me and visit a cat . . . ?

Astronomy Professor Bill Murray: Have fun and use protection.

[The entire class laughs.]

Later, Jason Schwartzman finds out that the older woman already knew him in the future before their "meeting" at Jimmy John's.

Jason Schwartzman: When you knew me in the future, was I still living in Sacramento?

Older Woman: Yes.

Jason Schwartzman, destroying his apartment in a rage: That's so fucked-up! I'm supposed to move to LA! The whole plan is to move to LA! This blows!

The older woman becomes stuck in the past because she can't afford a ticket back to the future (she's rich in the future but forgot to bring money with her to the present [her past]). She tries to come up with a plan to blackmail her rich father, but the plan doesn't work because she is—you see this fact reveal itself slowly as the film progresses—an idiot.

Jason Schwartzman: Maybe if you tell me some stuff about the future I can make bets and win enough money for you to go home.

Older Woman: Okay.

Jason Schwartzman: Who will be the next president?

Older Woman: Marc Summers.

Jason Schwartzman: Wait, the guy from Nickelodeon?

Older Woman: I guess. I'm not really into politics.

Jason Schwartzman: The guy from *Unwrapped* on Food Network?

Older Woman, becoming angry: I said I'm not into politics!

Jason Schwartzman: Okay. Take it easy. New idea. How about you ask your past self for the money?

Older Woman: I'm not rich yet in this timespace. I'll have to wait a few years.

They move to LA together so he can pursue his dream (owning a curry food truck) and she can avoid her past-life doppelgänger long enough so that the doppelgänger carries on her life as normal and isn't distracted from doing the thing that will ultimately make her rich (killing her dad in a car accident).

Suz was having a show in the Damhead Gallery on campus. Evidently gallery space was something you could just request as an undergrad, and if there was availability, then they let you have it. It was not a thing they advertised. To get it you had to be the kind of person who orders something that isn't on the menu.

Damhead was an irregularly shaped space, with a corner that wasn't visible from the entrance. You might not even register that the space turned a corner until you had turned around to leave.

Half the show was made up of six large paintings that hung on the two longest walls. The paintings consisted of heavy expressive black marks over finely detailed glossy floral backgrounds of blue and white and pinkish tan that looked like painted porcelain on stucco or something. In the weird corner of the room, against the thickly repainted white gallery walls, six TV monitors displayed live feeds of the paintings, where you could watch other people looking at the paintings, or people drinking wine in front of them, or nobody looking at them, offering a live feed of the painting, the screen framing it perfectly.

I was amazed by the paintings. The difference between the fine background detail and large-scale foreground brushstrokes vibrated back and forth and made me question the accuracy of my vision. I was always impressed by abstract stuff because I couldn't do it. Every time I tried, I immediately started seeing a figure, or a face, or a horizontal line that I couldn't see as anything but as a horizon line, and then the painting became that thing. What these paintings accomplished, in my opinion, was the way they made it difficult to see unintended shapes or figures. I could see only the brushstrokes on top of the porcelain and stucco textures. They did not mean more or less than that.

"I have the worst cramps," Suz said, joining me in front of the fourth painting. She dug through her backpack and brought out a bottle of Tylenol, took a few, and swallowed them with a gulp of red wine.

"I dropped a bottle of wine in the middle of the crosswalk on my way over here. It completely exploded in the street and got all over my boots and tights. The glass was in a million pieces and everyone was honking at me as I tried to figure out what to do and I just left all the glass there in the street. Well, I mean I picked up the largest piece of broken glass and then scurried away."

"Jesus. Are you okay?"

She lifted her leg to show me the wine splatter. I exaggerated my shock. It was only a little wine.

"I think it looks kind of cool actually," Suz said.

"I love these paintings," I said.

"Oh"—Suz waved flippantly at the paintings with the hand that wasn't holding a plastic cup of red wine—"these were just an idea I had randomly. They're not really the point of the show. I'm more interested in how viewers will react to seeing other people look at the art, and then realize that they were once the subject of the piece. I actually have secret cameras recording the second gallery area, to document people as they realize this."

"Right," I said. I closed my eyes and nodded in a way I had seen smart people do when in agreement with one another. I was disappointed in myself for being interested in the wrong part of the show.

Three women I vaguely recognized walked into the gallery and Suz left me to greet them. I poured wine into a plastic cup and went back to stand in front of *Painting 4*, which was my favorite. Thick, gritty strokes and messy blobs in salmon pink and hot pink and white, on a background made up of at least twenty different shades of black. I sat on my knees in front of it, knowing it would please Suz to have nontraditional gallery behavior showing on one of the screens, and attempted to draw the painting in my sketchbook.

I did a terrible job reproducing the painting. Suz's lines were elegant and confident. Mine were hesitant, sketchy, and broken in an overworked way, like when people try to mimic a child's drawing style.

I slept at Suz's apartment in Diana's bed. Diana was staying overnight somewhere. I slept in Diana's bed often, but this time I missed my apartment. I wanted to see my things. I wanted to smell my smells.

When I was little, I used to call home from my friends' houses after they fell asleep. Jenny would usually answer.

"What, you want Mom to pick you up?"

"No, I just have to ask her a question."

"I'm not giving her the phone until you admit you're a wussy little crybaby ding-dong head."

"I am that," I'd say, not wanting my friends to hear me call myself a wussy little crybaby ding-dong head.

"No. Say the whole thing or I'm not putting Mom on."

Diana's bed was larger than mine, and I spread my legs and arms out to form a big X. I closed my eyes and exhaled into air that seemed colder and fresher than the air in my own apartment.

"I am home," I said out loud into the air of Diana's bedroom, surprising myself, unsure of what I meant. Perhaps I was carrying out some fantasy laundry detergent commercial in which a woman feels most at home in clean laundry, no matter where she is. When the protagonist of the commercial exhales and says, "I am home," we (the viewer) can see only her face, smiling serenely, a generous stack of pillows behind her head, and an outline of her upper body beneath the blankets. The camera zooms out and we see that she is indeed on a bed (as expected), but that the bed is not in a similarly comfortable room, but rather outside at dusk. Zooming out farther, we see the house she was in has burned down, leaving only the foundation. The world outside her house, too, is a stark and craggy dystopian desert-scape. The foundations of other houses are scattered across the land like ruins. Something apocalyptic has happened, possibly not that recently. Malnourished, dying animals walk slowly by. Clearly they have no destination, but they're making an effort because pretending there is a chance for survival is what one does when faced with certain death. We snap back to a close-up of the woman as she lies in bed, blissfully unaware of the doomed world around her, lost in her clean, fresh, amazing laundry. That's how good this detergent is.

I texted my mom: *has Jenny come home?*

Several days later my mom texted: *whats the verizon pw again?*

I texted: *GooeyGumDrop8*

"If you won the lottery right now, would you continue working on the art you're currently working on?" Suz asked me.

We were sitting on blankets in Dolores Park, the sun blazing for once, our bikes stacked on the grass next to us. Suz lightly licked the joint she was rolling and smoothed it out.

"Hm," I said. It seemed like a trick question. If I won the lottery right now, wouldn't I have to fill out a bunch of forms to get the money? Then nervously wait for the money to arrive? I didn't think I could make art under those circumstances. And then I would want to spend some of my winnings immediately, in case there was an error and I had to give it back. Or I'd leave the country so the lottery people couldn't find me. I'd be on a beach in Thailand. I'd be on a beach in Spain. I'd be on a beach in Japan. I don't know, I'd like to see a beach. And of course I wouldn't take my *Rushmore* project with me. I'd probably forget all about it.

"If the answer is no, it was never art," she said.

"Is that from a fortune cookie?" I said.

She laughed heartily, unselfconsciously, sounding high already.

I didn't particularly like this park, and didn't understand why it was popular. It was always cold and there was always something disgusting in the grass. This time, for example, I saw what looked like a loogie with blood in it about a foot away from where our blanket ended. But I liked coming here with Suz, drinking beers from paper bags and talking shit about our peers and their bad art and bad hygiene and looking into the gray sky like it held answers.

"I wanted to become an artist because of MGMT," I said, attempting to be shocking.

Suz sputtered through the swig of beer she was currently swallowing and stared at me with faux outrage.

"Excuse me?" she said. She looked around, pretending to be worried that someone might have overheard me.

"I'm not ashamed to admit how deeply typical I am," I said.

"No, no, it's cool," Suz said, laughing. She lit a small joint and took a drag. "But I actually don't know if I'd classify that as typical."

"'Time to Pretend' specifically."

She laughed. I was enjoying embarrassing myself. It seemed to make Suz happy.

"Of course," she said, shaking her head. I started unpeeling a banana I had found unaccompanied in the student lounge earlier.

A man started digging through the trash nearby and then approached us, stumbling a bit. I noticed his big toes were sticking out of holes in each of his gray tennis shoes.

"Do you have a dollar?" he said.

"Sorry, I really don't," I said.

"I'm sorry," Suz said.

"No, *I'm* sorry," the man said angrily.

Things that can make you seem rich without lying and that cost nothing:

1. Not going straight to the snack table at an art opening, or avoiding the table the whole time you're there, or avoiding it until you're on your way to leave, picking up a single cracker on your way out.
2. Talking about your Mom's "summer home" (especially if you don't mention that it is also her autumn, winter, and spring home, and that she rents).
3. Casually saying you hate Paris and refusing to give a concrete reason why.
4. Mentioning your sister needs to go to rehab but excluding the fact that she'd definitely never have the money for that.
5. Not putting your phone in a protective case.

One year, when we were young, Jenny made Christmas cards for everyone in the family. The one she made for me depicted Santa bending over to take a shit near a fence of candy canes. I was impressed by the detailing in Santa's hands and boots, his expression, the haphazard coloring-in of his suit. I stared at it for hours, in awe of her skill. My own fine motor skills were not great, and I couldn't imagine having such control over a pencil.

"Draw me," I said. She drew me in bed with Landon, a boy who lived down the street whom I found disgusting, both of us smoking cigarettes. I understood the connotations and I hated it. She drew another on the back of the same piece of paper. This time Landon's genitals were exposed, and we had speech bubbles.

Landon's said, "That was great."

Mine said, "Can't wait to do it again."

There were hearts in my eyes and above my head.

I ripped it from her hands, worried our mom would see it, or that Jenny would find a way to show it to Landon, or somebody else who knew Landon, and it would be implied that this was a fantasy of mine. I needed to destroy it. Landon was disgusting. It was horrifying to see my own reality being torn down. These images were more real and tangible than my own feelings, the only evidence of them being my hysterical denial. The bedspread even looked like mine.

But for some reason, once I had the drawing in my possession, I didn't destroy it. I kept it. I moved it around to different hiding places on a somewhat obsessive weekly basis. I realized Jenny could make similar drawings with as much ease as she had made these first ones if she wanted to. Her talent was what I feared, not this particular drawing. Still, when I looked at it, I felt a wave of disgust as fresh as when Jenny showed it to me the first time. I was careful to fold it back up in exactly the same way so I wouldn't make more creases. It was the first piece of art that made me feel something.

It was hard to believe I'd only known Suz for less than a year. Sometimes it seemed like I could recall her in my childhood memories. It felt like she was with me on the playground, for example, chasing boys, pretending to be a horse. She was there, wasn't she, when Lindsay described a penis she saw on TV as "kind of a large thumb"? It didn't seem possible I had survived it all without Suz.

It was harder to transpose myself into Suz's memories, at least the ones I knew about. They were so outside of my experiences they may as well have taken place on another planet. For example, she had cheated on her boyfriend in high school, repeatedly, and lots of people knew and didn't tell the boyfriend. It's hard for me to even understand the completely foreign social dynamics that had made this situation possible:

1. Having a boyfriend.

2. Being so attractive and socially capable that two separate people wanted to sleep with you.

3. People respecting or fearing you enough to keep a secret they probably aren't explicitly being asked to keep.

She kept in touch with the guy she had cheated with. He went to Harvard to study film. They exchanged emails frequently and he sent her burned CD mixtapes and sometimes dick pics. I didn't understand any of these dynamics, either.

"I think I'm gonna pull an all-nighter tonight to finish this essay for Madness," I said. "If you want to join me." I swung a banana peel in front of us as if it were a temptation.

"Oh, that sounds rad. But I'm going to a poetry reading later with that chick Herta in Berkeley."

"Oh, I didn't know you, like, knew her at all?"

My chest felt hot and compressed, like something had been stolen from me while I wasn't looking.

"I don't. I ran into her at Pancho Villa the other day and we started talking about literature and she invited me to go see this New York poet who's doing a reading at Moe's Books. I should start heading over soon. I don't know how long it takes to get to Berkeley."

"Yeah," I said.

"What's the essay about?"

"What?"

"For Madness. That you have to write tonight."

"Oh. Schizophrenic visualizations. Van Gogh mostly." As soon as I heard myself say it, I realized how lame I sounded. Van Gogh? It was like I was trying to be as unimaginative as possible and pick up zero new art references while studying art at art school. Van Gogh.

Ever wonder if you picked Van Gogh because no one gives a shit if you can't come up with something original to say about him?

I tried to inhale deeply without making a sound, so that Suz wouldn't know I had lost my breath.

"Rad," she said again.

An opinion, not necessarily mine, but probably someone's, possibly someone smart and respected who has opinions that many people take seriously, potentially including myself, if I knew who this person was, or maybe it is even the opinion of many people all over the place for different reasons, maybe even a commonly held opinion, I have no idea: *The world needs bad art.*

Another opinion, this one definitely not mine, probably not anyone's, unless somebody for some reason widely and publicly asserted that no one held this opinion, in which case some other contrary person who was addicted to drama would probably claim that it was actually their firmly held opinion just to prove the first person wrong: *The world needs this particular bad art about* Rushmore, *a movie that the artist has not seen.*

If only I could afford therapy. Then I wouldn't need this art degree.

I walked around SFMOMA's pop art exhibition by myself. Museums are like a magic trick. Seeing paintings in a museum always sets a viewer up to find deep meaning and symbolism. The clean white walls. The placards. The seriousness. I tried to imagine I was walking around someone's dilapidated garage instead, viewing these same paintings. I guessed the art would feel less meaningful and important without the context of a fancy building.

Text to Suz: *Starting to think I'm the only one who doesn't like boring paintings*

Text to Suz: *I think I have a type of illness where I can only see flaws in things in the moment and years later I realize, in retrospect, that I liked something*

In high school, a pencil drawing of mine was accepted into the annual art show. It depicted Lindsay standing in front of A&W, the first full-body portrait I'd done. I'd been given an award at Assembly, and my drawing was hung in the Senior Hall for several weeks. I remember feeling much more proud of the drawing once I saw it hanging framed on the wall in a hallway where my classmates would pass it, than I had when I finished it alone in my living room in front of the TV.

When Jenny found out about it she said, "I'd be embarrassed to have my art on display like that. I wouldn't want everyone to think I thought I was better than them or something."

Text from Suz: *Philosophizing about the reasons you're a fucker doesn't make you any less of a fucker >:-)*

Me: *Obviously*

Me: *I know*

Me: *that*

On my computer, I searched "jennifer berry arrest" results for "past 24 hours" and found nothing. I expanded the search to "past week" and found nothing. I searched simply "jennifer berry" for "past week" and found nothing. I expanded the search to "past year" and found several results pertaining to Miss Oklahoma and Miss America.

I cried while Jenny was in labor. I was the only person with her at the hospital for most of it, and she was so vulnerable and beautiful that I momentarily forgot all the bad things I had ever thought about her. I held her hand. I felt nothing but love and admiration. I fed her ice chips from my fingers while she moaned. I texted her boyfriend Lucas from her phone to see if he was on his way. I texted our mom from my phone to tell her it was happening. I held my pee in so she wouldn't be alone even for a minute.

Then I watched a tiny person come out of her. It was like witnessing the future and the past at once, as though they were inextricable, woven together by an invisible cord that had always been there and always would be.

"Thank you so much for everything," she said to me afterward. We seemed to have both gotten to the same place of forgetting who we normally were to each other. "You're a good person. I love you."

"You're going to be such a good mom," I said, crying again. How long had it been since I looked closely at her? Said something genuine? Felt the warmth from her body?

I held the baby, who she named Brian Foley Cannon. I held him, kissed his forehead and his nose, stroked the white wispy hairs on his head, and promised him my everlasting love.

"The perfect baby boy," I told him.

"I'm guessing you want to move back in with me now?" Mom said loudly as she entered the hospital room, interrupting our tender moment. She dropped her giant purse onto a computer keyboard.

"Oh my god, Mom. Are you serious right now?" Jenny said. "My fucking ass is bleeding. I don't need this shit."

"Well, I assume you're not going to live on couches and street corners with a baby. I just don't know why any of this is my responsibility. You're an adult now. I don't see why you can't get your shit together. Ever."

She approached Brian, held his hand in hers, and cooed in baby talk, "You're pretty calm for a person entering this world without no place to live. You think your mom can turn her life around?"

I said, "They can use my bedroom. I don't really need it. I'll be going to college in a few months anyway."

"Oh, look who thinks they're the boss of my house. Maybe I wanted to use that room for when guests come over."

"Who?" I said. We hadn't been visited by anyone in years. Mom didn't answer me.

"Do you see the stupid shit I have to deal with, huh, little man?" Mom said to Brian in a singsong voice. "You're related to a lot of fucking assholes, I can tell you that right now. Yes, you are. Yes, you are."

"I swear to god, Mom," Jenny said. "Give me back my fucking baby."

"Where's your crackhead daddy anyway?" Mom said to the baby.

"He texted that he was on his way here," I said, happy to have something positive to contribute.

"Why are you looking at my texts?" Jenny said.

"You told me to text him."

"Yeah, I said, 'Send a text.' I didn't ask you to snoop around and read my messages and shit, you fucking weasel."

"Don't turn on me. I was here all day supporting you."

"You don't get credit for watching my anal sphincter throb for a few hours."

I let it go. Brian made a little cry, his chubby face surrounded by blanket. I felt a sharp and thick bulge in my stomach. Love? Fear? Something gastrointestinal?

"Your mom is just being a cunt bag to everyone around her, isn't she?" Mom cooed to the baby. "Yes, she is. Yes, she is, little man."

I spent the summer holding Brian's little head in my hand, making stupid noises at him, telling him all the good things that were likely to happen to him in his life.

"You're going to meet so many cool people, and go so many cool places with them, all over the world. You're gonna eat so much good stuff. Hear cool music and funny jokes. You're gonna have the best life."

I encouraged Jenny to take long showers so that I could say these stupid things to Brian privately.

"Where'd you get these foots? You stole these foots from me, didn't you? Didn't you? How could you? What am I supposed to do without my foots, you thief?"

Jenny softened in the weeks after Brian was born. We watched *SNL* and *The Real World* and *Survivor* on the new computer I bought for school. She reminisced about the spaghetti and meatballs Mom used to make for us sometimes. I looked up a recipe online, went to the store for the ingredients, and figured out how to brown meatballs by watching a video. Jenny and I ate while Brian slept next to us, wrapped in a thin white blanket Jenny stole from the hospital. He was impossibly peaceful, like the world would forever adapt to his needs and there would never be anything for him to worry about. Had we all begun life so confident that things would turn out well?

"So good," Jenny said. "Nothing like Mom's, but still, really good."

"I forgot to drop cigarette ash into the sauce," I said.

She laughed at my joke. "That must be it."

Brian woke up, also hungry. She continued to eat while feeding him, and I marveled at how Jenny could make up a whole human, a skeleton and organs and a thinking brain, using what she already had in her body. I wanted to tell Jenny I was proud of her for making a human. For using her body in such a profound way. Of holding him to her breast and continuing to build his body. *I'm proud of you*, I thought of saying. But it sounded stupid in my head, like the pointless drivel I'd say to Brian, so I said nothing.

"Is there more?" she said, handing me her plate.

"There is a lot more," I said.

If someone asks you for money and you don't give it to them

and then they start doing crack, you suspect in front of their kid, but you don't know for sure because you don't spend any time with them, and they ask you for money again

and you still don't give it to them

and they continue hanging out with their heroin-addicted home-less ex-boyfriend and panhandling for cash and stealing from the liquor store, and you know all this because you read the police re-ports from your shared hometown (you read these reports instead of calling) and they ask you for money again

and you still won't give it to them

not even ten dollars, not even five dollars, because you believe that once you give them money you will forever be their money person,

and you begin to pull away from them even more than you already had, and you stop reading the police reports because knowing about what's going on in their life makes you sad and ashamed in ways you don't want to confront at the moment

or maybe ever

and because you don't want to see yourself as someone who refuses to help someone who needs help, is begging you for help, that you *could* help if you chose to help but you won't help, because you have a vision of yourself as an artist, a successful one, one who likes what they do, and if you stop working toward that vision to help someone else, the vision will disappear and you will be left with nothing

then you just have to laugh

because isn't it funny how everything is ALWAYS ALWAYS ALWAYS ABOUT YOU?

yeast infection symptoms| 🔍

jobs that require no experience	history
what to do when no one wants to hire you	history
how to make $1800 last four months sa franciso	history
elvis pressely most famous song	history
elvis presley songs	history
what is loneliness called if you like it	history

close

"I've looked over my notes from Catie a bunch of times and this movie doesn't make sense to me. I don't understand what the plot is, or any of the characters' motivations or relationships to each other. How am I supposed to have a point of view about this project? What is any of this supposed to mean?"

"Yeah," Suz said.

"I feel so stupid. And I know for sure I'm going to make something I hate, so why am I even doing this?"

"Why don't you just make a film you actually want to make, and then figure out how it relates to *Rushmore* later? That way you're at least making something you like."

I nodded, pretending to consider this option. Did she think I had a bank of unused art ideas at the ready? It would be far easier to make something shitty that I hated based on ideas I had already started thinking about than come up with a completely new idea from scratch. But I knew not to say that. I was at least smart enough to know that "ease" should not be a determining factor in what art a person makes, at least not one they verbalize while paying a bajillion dollars to go to art school.

I said, "Someone had a cinnamon bun in class three days ago and I've been craving one ever since," and shortly thereafter Suz and I were in the darkened lot behind Whole Foods, opening the lid to a dumpster. Her idea, not mine. She had heard rumors that Whole Foods hadn't been locking their dumpsters. I guess the rumors were true.

I pushed a trash bag delicately to one side to look underneath it.

"We should have brought flashlights," Suz said.

I jumped into the dumpster and began fishing around more earnestly. It wasn't as gross as I'd imagined.

"Does dumpster diving make me look like a rich kid ironically overcompensating for their privilege?" I said, then felt ashamed for saying it, and worried that Suz would think that's what I thought about her.

She lifted her body up from the dumpster, victoriously holding a bouquet of flawless pink carnations.

"Nietzsche said that we should embrace our selfish desires," she said. "Society wants us to believe that desiring material wealth is bad so poor people won't form a revolution."

I showed her my findings: a dented can of chili.

We didn't find any cinnamon buns, but we did find another bouquet of carnations, a bag of smashed white bread, and a paper bag of bulk almonds with a grease spot on the bottom. As we sat on the ground divvying up our goods, a man appeared from out of nowhere, looming over us menacingly. I looked up into his face, which was angular, splotchy, sallow. I hit Suz on the arm, she hadn't yet noticed the danger we were in. Then *he* turned and ran away from *us*.

"What the hell," Suz said, laughing.

I laughed, too. We walked away from the dumpster, our backpacks full, a knot of guilt developing in my stomach. What I thought we were stealing from a major corporation with no moral compass we were in fact stealing from someone, a real person, with nothing at all.

Later, on the floor in my darkened apartment, surrounded by books, art supplies, thrifted furniture, nearly new, cheaply made textiles, and perfectly good almonds I had no intention of eating because the bag was dirty, I'd look up from the bright light of my phone and see my life in a way I hadn't before: as a gross display of wealth.

Artist's Assistant (mission district)

Are you looking for a fun, creative work environment?
I am a nationally showing artist looking for studio assistance.
Duties will include: Writing emails, studio cleanup, bringing
creative, inspiring energy to work with you every day, working
with sculptural materials (must have experience with wax and
plaster), taking out the trash (must be able to lift 50 lbs), written
and verbal communication with gallerists and buyers, extensive
art history knowledge, clean and tidy appearance, watching my
three children (5,7,8) from time to time, errands (must have own
car, preferably a truck or van), website and blog maintenance (and
regular communication with my web host), check writing and
light bookkeeping (knowledge about artist tax credits a huge plus),
ability to light and photograph sculptural work, enthusiasm for
simple tasks like coffee runs and vacuuming, and most importantly
a can-do attitude for anything else that might come up! Looking for
an intern needing school credit. Can't wait to meet you!

- Principals only. Recruiters, please don't contact this job poster.
- do NOT contact us with unsolicited services or offers

Suz and I got on the bus that would take us to the mall in Japantown. She wanted to buy a sake set for her mom, and she thought it was a good excuse to visit that part of the city. I'd never been there. The bus was crowded, so we sat across from each other, our backpacks in our laps. Suz put earbuds in her ears and turned around in her seat to look out the window. At every stop, the bus would almost fully clear out and then become crowded again with new passengers. I stared at her unabashedly, watched light flicker on the edges of her face; along the length of her nose, her stray baby hairs, the edges of her dark lashes.

Faces are language. They are poetry, interpreted differently by different people, beautiful to some but not others, more meaningful the longer you consider them. Instinctually, we believe a face can tell us a lot about who a person is. What we don't consider is that a face also holds clues for the person who owns it, clues that can help them understand who they are to the world.

Someone smells, I mouthed to Suz when she turned from the window and caught my eye. She smiled and shook her head. Then, looking around the bus, her face melted into terror. She looked down at her iPod, then up again at someone standing near her on the bus, then back to her iPod, over and over.

At the next stop, she gestured that we should get off the bus. As I waited to disembark, I looked around, wondering where the mall was. All I saw were apartment buildings.

"This isn't the right stop, but we're close enough," she said. "We can just walk the rest of the way. Is that okay?"

"Sure. You okay?"

"I thought I saw someone I recognized, but it wasn't him, but it freaked me out."

"Who?"

"This old art mentor. Fuck. It's kind of a long story," she said.

When Suz was fourteen, she got an apprenticeship with a printmaker named Soto. He had worked with many of Suz's mom's friends' kids over the years. He did all kinds of printmaking, but their focus together was mostly on screen printing, which is how he made a living. She'd go to his studio after school three days a week to learn how to design images, transfer the images to screens, print on various materials, etc. She developed a crush on Soto, who was in his early thirties and looked like David Bowie with piercings (left nostril and bottom lip—I asked). Her crush wasn't superserious, but it was enough to make her want to achieve greatness in printmaking, so as to impress him. She bought block printing supplies to use at home and, in the months after her apprenticeship ended, carved a series of full body nude self-portraits, mimicking the style of Albrecht Dürer, someone Soto had expressed admiration for several different times. This project was life changing for Suz. Her understanding of shape and light and composition developed dramatically over a short period. As she continued the series of self-portraits, her style moved away from mimicking Dürer into something her own, a style she couldn't grasp or identify as it was happening but that felt new and surprising. She started painting on the prints, watercolor washes and thick lines of acrylic thickened with mediums and careful detail work to deepen parts of the prints. She understood she was feeling artistic inspiration, a propulsion to move forward with these ideas, not knowing where they were going to take her. She had never felt that before.

"Then we learned that Soto had been arrested on child pornography charges," she said. "It all suddenly felt very crumbly and meaningless."

Soto had inspired this new direction in Suz. She felt that without working with him, she may not have gotten to a place where she felt obsessed with and fulfilled by art. Her dad had been encouraging her to go into finance, and maybe she would have taken that direction in life if not for Soto, who had, she found out from a news segment, kept images of children on the same computer she used while working with him.

Suz wanted to quit art. She wanted to untangle herself from the darkness of Soto. She blamed herself for not seeing what he was, for having a crush on him, for wanting to impress him, for carving her own nude figure, hoping one day he would see it and be impressed.

"The thing is, I wasn't a victim. In some ways I wanted to be. I wanted to be like, *Oh, poor me, my artistic identity will forever be wrapped around a pedophile. And on top of that my taste in men is a huge cause for concern.* But there were actual children being hurt. And, really, I had only benefitted from knowing Soto. Whatever his sick, fucked-up role in the world was, I had grown and changed in positive ways because I was inspired by aspects of his work."

We walked in silence for a few minutes as I panicked about the fact that I didn't know what to say.

"That's dark," I said, immediately embarrassed at my inclination to sum up the mood of her experience.

"Extremely dark," she said. "Fuck, now I'm back in that place of feeling like I didn't do enough to help anyone."

I could see that it was a difficult thing for her to go through, and I wouldn't want to have been close to someone who did what Soto did, but I couldn't muster any sorry feelings for Suz. I kept focusing on the wrong details. A mentor who was a professional artist. Two parents who showed an interest in her life. The ability to buy all new art supplies in a different medium on a whim at age fourteen. A little guilt in exchange for all of that wasn't a bad trade-off.

We walked through a brightly lit, sparsely inventoried ceramic store in the mall, touching small glazed dishes until we found the aisle with sake bottles and cups. They looked like dishes for dolls. Suz picked out a black bottle with four comically tiny cups that cost about the same amount as my art supply budget for the entire semester.

Suz suggested we go to a restaurant for ramen before heading back to the bus stop. I didn't want to spend money eating out, but I figured ramen couldn't be more than a few dollars. I guess I severely underestimated the price range of curly noodles in water. I ordered the least expensive thing on the menu, which was ramen with scallions and corn for eight dollars, the cost of approximately twenty-five instant ramen meals. I decided not to worry about the money, since I was partially doing this to make Suz feel better. In a perfect world, I would have offered to pay for Suz's lunch, too, but Suz ordered an expensive ramen that came with meat and runny eggs, as well as a spicy tuna roll.

Suz quietly looked into her water cup as we waited for our food. I seemed to be disappointing Suz, not knowing how to talk about hard things, not saying anything comforting, not helping in any way.

I'm sad, too, I wanted to say. I wished she could see inside me without my having to say anything.

"What happened to that guy, Soto?" I said.

"As far as I know he's in prison," Suz said. "But I haven't looked him up in a while. He could be out. It would be so fucked to run into him. Anyway. Let's talk about something else."

We sat silently for a few moments.

My sister is missing, I could say. *She left her baby son with our mom, who can't afford childcare for him while she's at work.*

Or I could say, *It's strange to feel both close with someone and like you never knew them. It does make you feel like a bad person. That is a feeling I can relate to.*

"How's your *Rushmore* thing coming along?" she said.

"Oh, wow. I forgot all about that."

"Oh," Suz said, somewhere else again, looking down into her water cup.

If I brought up my sister, Suz might think I was trying to compete with her story. She could also feel judged, like I was comparing her passing ignorance to my ongoing lack of interest in helping my family. It was probably better to move on from sad topics.

"Ew, it's raining," I said.

Suz turned her head to look out the window and didn't turn it back until our food came.

Rushmore (2011 Joelle Berry remake)

Jason Schwartzman, riding a bike down a quiet residential street in what appears to be the middle of the night. He is wearing a suit and a beret and has a backpack.

Jason Schwartzman voice-over: I don't know why I do this. I guess there is something in me that feels I need to compensate for all the bad things I've done in my life. Not that I've done a lot of bad things. I mean, who hasn't done bad things? Who hasn't wished for the death of a loved one, only accidentally and only for a second? Who hasn't wished for someone else's life to be easier, not for that person's sake, but so that one wouldn't have to worry so much about them? But I'm trying to be better.

Jason Schwartzman leans his bike quietly against a fence in a dark alley, climbs through a gap between the fences of one property and another, and quietly tiptoes over to a dark house.

The voice-over continues: When Kira was in high school, she asked a mentally disabled boy to be her prom date. Her community was so proud of her for this. They wrote about her good deed in the paper. That's when I first set eyes on Kira, seeing her beautiful smiling face on the third page of that paper underneath the article about how the only gas station in town had been revealed to be a drug front, her arm around that boy who I presumed she did not have romantic feelings for but maybe she did. Teenage girls are not as one-dimensional as people believe. Kira certainly wasn't, isn't, could never be. Kira has many dimensions, all of them vitally important to me.

Jason Schwartzman produces a single key from his pocket, quietly un-
locks the back door of a house, and then takes out a strip of dog jerky
from his other pocket, which is then immediately handed to a dog
that is waiting next to the door inside the home. He tiptoes carefully
past the dog into the house, a small, dated kitchen with a stone fruit
theme. He closes his eyes and inhales deeply, then continues tiptoeing
quietly farther into the house.

The voice-over continues: I consider it my job to protect Kira from
every mistake, every setback, and every minor inconvenience. I've
fixed leaks, called her employers to praise her customer service,
and even disappeared a bad, bad dude that was interfering with her
happiness.

Jason Schwartzman enters the bathroom, slowly unzips his backpack
and extracts two large rolls of toilet paper. He opens the cupboard
under the sink and places them there, one on top of the other. The dog
emerges and Jason Schwartzman seamlessly hands him another strip
of dog jerky. Then he slowly makes his way back through the house
toward the back door he entered from, pats the dog on the head before
closing the back door silently.

The voice-over continues: Kira doesn't know about any of this. She's
never even seen my face. But I live my life in service to her. Her
happiness is all—

Jason Schwartzman squeezes through the gap in the fence and sees
Bill Murray standing ominously next to Jason Schwartzman's bike.

Bill Murray: I know what you've been doing. And I want to be part
of it.

In Madness we had a lecture about Richard Dadd, who was an example of an artist with mental illness (likely schizophrenia), as well as an example of an artist who made work about mental illness, despite believing his whole life that he did not have mental illness. We learned he killed his own father, believing him to be the devil.

There was an exhibition happening in the gallery next to the classroom Madness was held in, and the sounds of people talking and moving around and eating turkey rollups (I had seen them being arranged as I entered class) spilled into our room, which was darkened and quiet for the slide presentation.

"Astounding," I heard someone say, rising above the din.

My favorite slide of Dadd's was one called *The Child's Problem*, featuring an absolutely terrifying young child playing chess in front of a sleeping old woman.

"Oh my god. I love your boots," I heard someone say.

"The shocking depiction of a lifelong battle with madness," our professor said about the painting. I didn't buy it. The fact that the artist was suffering mental illness didn't necessarily mean all of his work was about that mental illness. Anyway, if he didn't even believe he had mental illness, why would he make art about having it? The piece seemed to me to be more about the terror of childhood, the monstrosity of a child's place in the world. Being small and stuck in a world that wasn't built for you, a world you have to find a way to exist within forever, a reality even more painful and impossible than it sounds.

"An unsettling composition pointing with an odd perspective, obscuring the entire body of the main figure," our professor was saying.

I shrugged and rolled my eyes, realizing while doing it that people could see me. I nodded and pursed my lips in agreement with myself that I would try to stop having physical reactions to my private critical thoughts.

I scanned the room and made eye contact with a guy across from me named Micah, who was smiling at me mischievously.

After class, I walked through the gallery next door. It was a group show from an illustration class, and the quality of the work was extremely varied.

There weren't any turkey rollups left.

There was a large white piece on the far wall with black marks that I couldn't make out from across the room. The composition felt familiar, like a page from a notebook kept beside the landline. As I got closer I realized it was a giant screen print that was, or was meant to look like, a blown-up diary entry. At the top, in the swirling, chaotic penmanship of a little girl, it read, *Chase Cunningham has a crush on me NO*. Below it was more text that read, *makin me quesy*, next to a drawing of a heart with an X over it. And at the bottom of the piece, a drawing of a heart with a face and vomit spewing from its mouth and next to it yet another heart with a speech bubble that read, *more like chase you away, chase*. I looked at it for a long time, having short bursts of the specific feeling of being seven and eight, newly identifying my feelings about being looked at by my peers, desired by them, or repulsed, my own desire and repulsion mixed up in those feelings in confusing ways, the playfulness of it all in retrospect, the slow and steady way that playfulness disappeared and became dead serious.

I noticed the tag and saw that it was made by Diana.

I thought about how Diana had sat down next to me and tried to talk to me about her parents. I had felt so impatient, irritated by her assumption that I was interested in her. But this print was another way of talking to me about herself, and I felt open to it and connected to the feelings it presented. That Diana was once a child who understood little about her place in the world was (1) somehow new information and (2) somehow made me like her more.

I was a little girl once, too, I thought dumbly.

I stared at the barfing heart and tried to pinpoint what it made me feel. There were so many hearts for something that claimed to dismiss the idea of love. So much emotion wound up in rejecting an emotion.

I received a text from an unknown number. *Hey, this is Micah from madness. I got ur number from the class roster hope that's not weird. Would u want to go to a show with me tonite?*

I texted: *Micah from madness would be a cool band name*

Then I texted: *Sure*

He texted: *lol right on*

I met Micah at Sixteenth and Mission, then we walked to the show together. The show was in the back of an old furniture store that had been gutted, and we were a little bit late. Micah pulled warm beers out of his backpack, handed one to me, and led me into the crowd to watch a guy with a synthesizer and a drum machine sing a song about something being not okay.

This is not okay, this is not okay, the song went. It was like watching someone perform therapy on themselves. I wanted to look away but the only lights on in the venue were pointed at him. I kept thinking, *This used to be a furniture store,* which made the show more tragic. After "This Is Not Okay," the performer thanked the crowd for coming and apologetically informed us that there would be one more song before he left the stage.

His next song was a little more upbeat in tempo and went, *I should have known you'd, nothing, never mind. Nothing, never mind. Well actually, yeah, no, never mind. It's nothing. Don't worry about it. Don't worry about it. Don't worry about it.* His voice went into an increasingly high falsetto for the last few lines.

"Does this guy need help?" I yelled to Micah. He laughed.

"What's this band called again?"

"Landon Grace," Micah said.

I felt drawn to the performer. I felt bad for not liking the songs, for being another person (of many, I guessed) his work failed to move. His failure to move me somehow made me like him. Failure was a common ground, perhaps.

Micah woo'd sarcastically when the song ended and I smiled at the performer in case he looked out into the crowd, which he did not. We watched him start to take down his equipment.

"Was that, like, a joke set?" Micah said, a little too loudly.

It felt plausible that the performer's intention was to make me feel worried that he felt rejected and bad about himself because of the poor crowd reaction, and that he might throw himself off a building because of it. I watched him struggle with taking his microphone off its stand until it popped off suddenly and hit him in the chin.

I felt a love for the performer that felt familiar. I wanted him to disappear so that he wouldn't be subjected to the ridicule directed at him. I wanted to tell him his art was good, so that he would believe at least one person thought so. I wanted to hold him like a baby.

"God, I feel weird now," I said.

"Sorry, I thought that would be cool," Micah said.

Micah fell off his skateboard outside of the venue and landed on the road into oncoming traffic. I laughed, suspecting that embarrassing him would make him want to come to my apartment. It worked, and he came over. He made fun of the Vans sticker on my laptop, took off my underwear, and gave me the worst oral sex of my life.

Of my life.

It made me feel sorry for his ex-girlfriend, whom I knew he had been with for several years until recently because he had mentioned this a bunch of times over the course of the night.

"It's on and off," he had said, which evoked a light switch clicking back and forth. The inevitability of it being turned in the opposite direction again, at some point, made me relax. I was some kind of a decorative novelty lamp, not his main light source. But it did hurt my feelings that his ex-girlfriend hadn't taught him oral sex.

I felt bad about the oral sex the next day and was even spiraling into a low-grade depression because of it. It was so bad I was sort of inspired. It was like this huge phenomenon I discovered.

There should be a tv show about the terrible oral sex Micah gives, I texted Suz. *Its . . . amazing.*

Then I remembered that part of why I was feeling so bad was that my sister might be dead (*I'm not that lucky*, my brain kept saying in the voice of Buzz McCallister, trying to comfort me) or hurt, or in trouble. And that even if she was okay, her small son would have to live in a world where his mom might leave him any moment. The unfairness was unbearable, and I ached for the ability to protect him.

I tried, then, to focus on Micah's bad oral sex. A calming problem, really, one that didn't have to be a problem at all. I could simply, if I wanted to, never see Micah again. Or I could seek him out as a way to control the type of pain I felt, his terrible oral sex a lesser, lighter pain I could use as a distraction from far worse feelings.

If I'm not evil, then why do I fantasize about taking care of Brian, loading his things into a suitcase, taking him on the bus, and moving him to my tiny apartment, finding a way to balance making art and finding childcare and ever-increasing San Francisco rents and everything, making him my baby, becoming our own family unit?

If I'm not evil, then why does this fantasy end the moment I imagine that Jenny is alive? Why do I want to help only if it doesn't benefit my sister?

"How would I know if I'm evil or not?" I said.

Suz looked at me with tenderness and affection, a slight smile thinning her lips, and said, "Why would you be evil? Because you don't recycle?"

Studio Manager (potrero hill)

Ever feel like your boss doesn't understand you? Do you want to work in a collaborative, artistic environment? Do you want more from a job than just a paycheck?

Apply now to be the Studio Manager for a thriving Arts community! You will oversee all the comings and goings of our bright, light-filled studios and keep our workspaces in tip-top shape. Your duties include: receiving deliveries, keeping our kitchen clean and the coffee hot, nightly studio cleaning, taking out garbage, separating recyclables from garbage (you will do this outside by the dumpster as there is nowhere to do it in the studios), keeping the bathroom tidy, using only earth-friendly cleaning supplies (you will supply), and participation in monthly meeting about studio needs (this meeting will not be paid but someone usually brings doughnuts).

We are looking for someone with an MFA with a focus on Painting and/or Printmaking (in case one of us needs you for help on a project!). Follow the link below to take a personality test to see if you are a good fit!

- Principals only. Recruiters, please don't contact this job poster.
- do NOT contact us with unsolicited services or offers

I invited Suz over but she said she had already promised Diana a girls' night, so I invited them both over.

They brought a jar of face mask cream and organic corn chips and oven-baked potato chips and a jar of queso to my apartment. I played *Æon Flux* from my laptop for background noise and we all sat on the floor eating snacks, putting our faces into a haircut generator I found online, and trying to find embarrassing photos of our classmates on our phones. It was the perfect night, and I felt guilty that I was having such a good time, that peace and lightness were so easily attainable for me when I knew that my mom's plans for the night were washing Brian's poopy overalls in the kitchen sink because her washing machine was broken and then calling the police station to see if they had any information about my missing sister. I almost wished things weren't so easy for me, and then felt sad for myself that I would feel guilty about my own happiness.

But what was my other option? Wishing for happiness for my family was too easy a wish, too out of my control to waste energy on. Nothing I did could make them happy, but their unhappiness was made worse by my actions: my insistence on moving away from Lodi and living in a place just the right distance away that I would conveniently be unable to help. And my own moments of happiness or success seemed to cause unhappiness for them as well. What choice did I have but to wish for my pleasures to be modest and infrequent and so borderline positive that I could easily still spin them into negatives so as not to inflict pain on my family?

"My apartment is really cold so sometimes I sleep in my painting studio," I'd said to my mom, too ashamed to admit I loved the painting studios and enjoyed working so late into the night that it didn't make sense to go home and come back again for my morning class.

In *The Conversation*, extreme guilt doesn't stop Gene Hackman's character from being involved in the things that cause him guilt. It only stops him from enjoying anything about his life.

"Queso should be, like, criminal," Diana said, stuffing a handful of broken potato chips into her mouth. I loved Diana for saying that, for saying things that weren't meant to make me feel bad for her, or make me feel anything in particular, and for being in my apartment instead of all the other apartments she could be in, and for her simple desire to have a fun night, and allowing me to be included in it. And I hated her, too, for all those same things, for the way they represented the good fortune she'd experienced in her life, how that fortune formed her impression of the world and that made her someone who was easy to hang out with. And I was fortunate for knowing her, and it was annoying that I had to be appreciative for things Diana probably never even thought about. How wide the gap was between our understandings of the world.

And why, by the way, was she reaching back through the wrong end of the gap, to spend an evening with me?

"I could call the cops if you want," I said. I sounded a little more threatening than I had intended. Diana smiled generously, chip crumbs falling into her lap.

Suz turned off *Æon Flux* and turned on ambient music without asking me, not as a power move, but seemingly completely unaware that it might bother someone to change shared media without discussion. But did it actually bother me or was I just bothered by the fact that she didn't realize that someone might be bothered? Was I bothered by the idea that to her, the collective agreement of shared media was an issue of little importance, but to me, control of the remote had always been a huge source of familial conflict? That had to be what my problem was about, because I didn't care if *Æon Flux* was on or not. I had no problem with the ambient music. I just felt like my entire existence, everything I had grown up knowing about the world, about myself, about social hierarchy, was being disregarded.

I had to excuse myself so I could quietly rage about my wildly lopsided expectations of reality in my bathroom. I stood in front of the mirror. I had scary eyes, I noticed. Eyes that conveyed deadness. The kind of eyes that failed to express emotion. I visualized tearing them out of my skull with my fingers. I realized I wasn't breathing and gasped for air. Having fun with my friends was giving me spontaneous, hot terror.

I turned the faucet on and put my hands under the cold water. I stared at my fingers in an effort to avoid eye contact with myself. I briefly considered the history of the universe, how an enormously large number of random events had led to my existence, and then another unfathomably large number of random events led to the nature of my personality, the ability to look at myself and see deadness and feel ambivalence about it. To be like, *maybe dead eyes are a gift.*

I left the bathroom and returned to my place on the floor. Diana had produced a giant bag of nail polish and started painting her fingernails primary blue in a shockingly careless manner, brushing the nail and also all the skin around each nail with paint, without the slightest indication that this was not her intention. I had never seen anyone paint their nails like this before. Did excess polish peel off the skin after a couple washes, leaving a perfect manicure? Had I been careful my whole life for no reason?

"I have some mushrooms we can do later if you guys want," Suz said.

"Oh, okay," I said, the hot terror returning to my chest and throat. I immediately thought of Jenny. No particular memory, just the fact of her existing, or not, somewhere in the world. My moral judgment against almost everything she did. Her drug use as a flaw I felt she had picked out for herself from a shelf of more desirable flaws. My inability to see her as a complex and wounded person with conflicting desires and few options.

But I wanted to do mushrooms, actually. I was curious about what a hallucination would feel like. What visions would come to me? What artistic revelations would transpire? Would I finally relax?

After all the headshaking about my sister, here I was, ready to experiment with drugs.

But Suz didn't bring it up again and we ended up watching a film about the oppression of Native Americans that Suz's mom's friend had produced.

Sexual Fantasy

Him, in my apartment, paint smeared excessively on his face, possibly purposefully, after a long day in the studio: As a young middle-class white male, I am more primed for success than almost everyone else around me.

Me: [Pretending to read Kafka]

Him: Even though almost everyone else around me is much more interesting than I am. And also more talented and deserving of success.

Me: Mmhmm.

Him: I should just quit making art, right?

Me: [Pretending to read the same page I've been pretending to read for three days]: It's too late to quit art.

Him, confidently: It's never too late to quit art.

[I finally look up from my book]

[Sex]

Professor Herrera told me I should think more broadly about my project.

I had gone to her office hours to complain about my lack of progress with *Rushmore* and the obstacles I had set up for myself. The financial restraints, for one, though not intentional, were unavoidable, given my student status and lack of access to locations and wardrobe and movie stars and things like that.

Herrera's office was a gray box. It had one window, looking out into a parking lot for a plastic fabrication business. There was no art, or photos, or even any framed credentials. I wondered if she shared this office with a lot of other professors.

"I have a few other ideas. Maybe I don't have to go through with this?" I said. I gestured at my backpack, where I had a list of other ideas I was hoping to be invited to explain.

"You don't need to tie yourself to your original conception in a literal sense. Be open to the idea shifting and growing. Think of the *Rushmore* concept as a set of building blocks you can move around, put in a different order, or disguise as something else."

It made some sense. I could imagine this working with another kind of project. But I couldn't figure out what it meant for this one.

"I don't have to re-create *Rushmore* necessarily, literally, but something more broad . . ." I trailed off so Herrera could jump in and finish my sentence for me if she wanted. "More broadly, like, work with the concepts that come up in talking to people about the film . . ." I didn't know what I was saying.

"Exactly," she said. "Sure."

I nodded.

"Have fun with it," she said encouragingly, like she was talking to an elementary school student. "The point of this project is to get you thinking conceptually. You don't have to be in love with the final product. It's about the ideas you're working with, what those ideas symbolize to you, and how you're choosing to convey those symbols."

I nodded.

"Does that make sense?" she said.

"Yeah, totally." I wanted to leave her office, run the mile and a half to my apartment, take off all my clothes, and rub chunky peanut butter onto my stomach, as a symbolic gesture indicating my deep lack of comprehension regarding this conversation.

"Thank you for your time," I said.

I don't know if I like art or if I've found the one thing you can be interested in without liking.

I have always had a deep desire to be a "regular" somewhere. I wanted to be the type of person who would go to a bar or restaurant so often that when I walked up to the counter, the cashier would say, "The usual?" and some other employee, having seen me come in and knowing my order by heart, would have my chicken salad sandwich or whatever ready before I even paid. But I couldn't afford to go anywhere frequently enough that employees could come to know me. Instead, I decided I'd be a regular at this one particular bench in the main hallway.

"Joey! Hey! Want to sign up for the craft fair?"

I turned to see Allen walking toward me with a clipboard.

"It takes place the last weekend before the end of the semester, and it's a chance to show off all that you've—"

"I don't really have anything . . . No, I don't think so," I said, trying to keep a pleasant expression despite the awfulness of the invitation.

Allen smiled warmly, as if I had complimented him on his thoughtfulness. "That's okay. If you change your mind, let me know! It's still two months away."

He handed me a postcard-sized flyer advertising the craft fair, and I reached for it in slow motion, hoping some external force would intervene before it touched my fingers.

Allen's enthusiasm didn't seem appropriate on an art school campus. I would have preferred the student body cheerleader (or whatever his job was) to be a little more dour, to stand in corners smoking a cigarette and nodding toward the craft fair sign-up board while rolling his eyes.

"Maybe," I said. "Let me see." And then I gestured in the direction I was walking, indicating nothing.

The end result of my *Rushmore* remake is either a success or a failure

And therefore both simultaneously

And nothing in between

Which is comforting in the way

I don't understand quantum theory

So it can't hurt me

I decided to invite Micah over to my apartment. I didn't want his terrible oral sex, so I turned on a documentary about viruses.

He left partway through the film, claiming his roommate was locked out of their apartment.

The viruses seemed endearing, and I was rooting for them by the end.

personality test correct answers| 🔍

jobs for artists	history
jobs for artists that pay	history
are white stripes band breaking up	history
has wrong interpretation of movie ever ruined someones life	history
peanut butter recipes	history
absurdism albert camus	history
free art supplies	history
art history marilyn stokstad full text free online pdf	history

close

I walked to school, entered the student café with a degree of confidence I almost never possessed, dispensed brewed coffee into my thermos like it was owed to me, poured cream into the coffee from the carafe by the microwave, and turned around and walked away from the coffee station trying my best not to look in the direction of the cash register, which I knew would make me look weak, invite interrogation, and cost me two dollars.

Suz was at one of the café tables with a slice of quiche.

"Have you ever wanted to go to Burning Man?" she said.

"I'm going to pretend I didn't hear that," I said.

"You wouldn't even want to go so you'd have a basis for your judgment against it?"

"I don't have any judgment against Burning Man, I just think all the most awful people go to it and do the stupidest shit I can imagine so that they can feel cool for five days before they go back to their stupid tech jobs and ruin the planet."

"You're so unreasonable," she said.

"Now I'm mad," I said. "You love to rile me up."

"I really do," she said.

I noticed Benji in line at the café. Benji was someone I had kissed at a dorm party first semester of first year. I had decided I wanted to kiss him after I heard him say that the most difficult part of college so far had been the fact that there were no bathtubs in the communal dorm bathrooms. I made sure I was standing near him all night until I found a moment where we happened to both be standing alone and near each other.

"Where are you from?" I had said.

"Tulsa," he said. And then pretty much right after that we were making out.

After that he'd knock on my dorm room door once in a while and ask me to hang out. I usually didn't want to hang out, so I usually didn't. But then he stopped trying, and I missed the attention.

I smiled at him now, and he pretended he didn't see me. Feeling aggressive, I loudly said, "Hi, Benji."

"Oh hi, Joey," he said. His mouth curled into an enormous smile that dug deeply into his dimples. He continued walking past us. I remembered with sudden clarity that his mouth had tasted like butter garlic sauce from Domino's. It had made me hungry then and it was making me hungry now remembering it.

"Who is that?" Suz said while he was possibly still in earshot.

"Oh, this guy Benji I hung out with a couple times. He's such a fucking idiot it's almost sexy," I said.

"I've never understood the concept of having sex with someone you can't have a conversation with," she said.

"You can have a conversation, it just has to be like, [idiot voice] *What's a microwave actually do? Dude, I don't know.*"

"Okay, yes, that sounds hot."

I saw my mom was calling and, since I was wasting time walking through the student galleries between classes, I picked up the phone.

"Hi, honey. How are you? I have an insane migraine. I just wanted to call you real quick and let you know my neighbor Allison has been taking care of Brian for me while I'm at work. I still haven't heard from Jenny."

I wondered how long it would take for one of us to broach the topic of whether Jenny was still alive or not. Days? Weeks? Years?

"Okay," I said. "Is that the same neighbor as before? Is she okay? Like not on drugs or anything?"

"She's okay. Brian likes her. She wants fifty dollars a day though. I don't know why I should have to deal with this. I have enough going on."

I walked out of the galleries and into the main hallway to try to find somewhere where nobody would overhear my conversation.

"Sorry. It's really unfair. I don't know why Jenny is so irresponsible."

"Can you try to call Jenny again? Her phone was going straight to voicemail for a while but now it's ringing but she's not answering."

"Yeah, I can call in a few," I said, feeling like I already knew the end of the story.

When I was eleven, I always wanted to go to Claire's at the mall, to look at earrings and bracelets. At some point, Jenny started going into the store with me. I was annoyed because I guess I thought mall jewelry was *my* thing?

I stole a Capricorn symbol necklace, just put it on and wore it out of the store.

I desperately wanted to be a Capricorn. I thought moodiness and depression looked more sophisticated on Capricorns, and astrology books seemed biased in favor of them. I wanted badly to be accepted by the astrology community, and I liked goats.

Okay? I liked goats.

Being a Capricorn isn't something you can steal for yourself, however, and that fact weighed on me. I didn't have the innate traits, the raw determination or whatever, the goatiness about myself.

I know this doesn't have anything to do with Jenny.

I have a hard time thinking about Jenny without redirecting my thoughts to myself.

I believe our DNA is so different from each other's that, if studied, it could scientifically prove that "family" is a meaningless construct made up by animals to get humans to herd them.

She could have been an artist. I likely wouldn't have thought to make art myself if she hadn't been good at it first. But being good at something isn't enough for some people.

I didn't want to draw when Jenny was home. She could draw, too, I knew. I didn't want to share that with her. I hid my drawings in my Earth Science textbook, a competitive move. If she didn't know I was drawing, she wouldn't remember to practice herself. But it was possible she was drawing in secret, too, I thought. Maybe she was trying to be better than me, and that's why she stayed out late most nights, or didn't come home at all, because she was practicing drawing in secret. I really thought everything was about me.

She is a Sagittarius, which reminds me how little I actually care about astrology, how boring it is unless it's about me.

I wanted her to be okay, but like, I'd only say it while sighing so everyone knew it was a burden for me to worry about her.

When I was eleven, Jenny was fourteen, and since we shared a room I could see and hear and even smell her boyfriend, who came to her window some nights and helped her down off the ledge onto the outside of our trailer.

She didn't try to hide any of this from me. She didn't turn around at the last second and whisper, *Tell Mom and you're dead.* She just slid away.

It was as if I wasn't even there.

I had a dream my
life wasn't
pointless and my
family wasn't holding
me down and I was
getting a degree in
something that
mattered and
I didn't have a cowlick
on my forehead.

Leaving Art History, my last class for the day, I received a text from Jenny: *Can you wire me 500 to walgreens in reno?*

I texted: *What where are you?*

I sat on the bench in front of the drawing studios and waited for a response. I thought about texting Mom immediately, letting her know I had heard from Jenny, but I decided to wait to get more information.

I called Jenny, but she didn't answer.

She texted: *Reno. Im stuck here. I need money for a hotel I havent slept in like five days lol I lost my shoes an spent my last 20 bucks on flip flops*

I texted: *Why are you in Reno?*

After a few minutes, she texted: *This guy said he could get me a job so we hitchhiked outhere together then he ducking left me just disap-peared. An of course there aint no job. Fucking lowlife. I told him I had a kid an cant leave lodi unless it was for legit work. He was bein all lovey dovey an shit. Told me we were gonna make a life togther. turns out he has a ducking wife in truckee lol*

I stared at my phone.

What about 100? she texted after I hadn't responded for a couple of minutes.

I texted: *I cant. Are you going home? Mom is freaking out*

It started to rain. I got mad at myself for forgetting my rain gear. My studio apartment was a ten-minute bike ride away. I'd have to choose to either get drenched on the way home or stay on campus until my next class three hours later.

There was no reply from Jenny.

"Why did you choose to only paint men?" Kevin said.

"Is this an artistic question or a political question?" Herta said.

"Isn't everything political?" Kevin said. Another male student agreed with him by saying, "Mmm," loudly.

"Do you actually want to know my artistic reasons for painting men," Herta said, "or is this your sexist way of telling me I need to conform to some preconceived notion of what subjects and themes you think have artistic merit?"

"I'm just asking because it's obviously a choice you made and I wonder what your thoughts are about it."

There was a Kmart a couple of miles from where we lived and often my senior year of high school, having nothing to do after school or on a weekend, I would walk there, vaguely hoping to see my classmates there with their parents.

I always had money at that point, though my mom and sister didn't know it. I was starting to understand that money held great power, greater than just the power of being able to buy things. I opened a bank account and kept the card in a hidden zippered pocket inside my backpack.

On one such trip, as I walked toward the entrance of Kmart, I saw Jenny panhandling with a sign that read, *Anything helps. Jesus Bless.*

"Jen?" I said.

"Joey! Do you have five dollars you can give me?"

"No. What are you doing?"

"Forget it," she said, folding her sign and shoving it under her armpit. She stood up from the curb and walked away from me toward the back of the store.

"Jen!" I yelled. She ignored me.

I walked around inside Kmart for some time, wondering how often Jenny was outside of Kmart asking for money and looking around for people I recognized, and eventually decided to buy some body lotion.

I saw Jenny sitting outside of a gas station with her sign on my way home, though I didn't approach her, and I don't think she saw me.

"It doesn't matter if they're men or women," Herta said. "That is my point. You see all men, I just see people. You are the one bringing sexism into this. You don't ask why male painters have only painted female subjects."

"You don't know what I ask male painters. You're projecting sexism onto me."

The image of Jenny sitting in front of a Kmart has stuck with me, because from that moment forward, I was someone who would watch their sister beg for money while clutching a twenty-dollar bill I had no designated need for. I've always wondered if that was a choice I made or an innate feature of my personality.

I'd started working for my friend Lindsay's grandma Carol the summer before twelfth grade. Carol was a watercolorist with a focus on

terribly boring seaside landscapes. She was something of a Lodi fix-
ture, and her work made the rounds in the local galleries, in both
solo and group shows. She showed the same pieces over and over. It
seemed odd to me at the time, but when I asked her about it she said
that's what all artists did. There was one small painting in particular
that I hated, depicting a small cottage in an open field, not even a
tree or shrub to keep the cottage company. Not even a flower. *This
landscape needs a landscaper,* I had thought.

Carol liked to think of me as her protégé, and herself as my mentor.
I'd go to her house and we'd watch *Maury* together in her painting studio, which doubled as a dining room, and which also had a
treadmill.

She'd tell me the monetary value of her paintbrushes, sketch and
erase and sketch and erase a horizontal line on Bristol board, tell
me the cost of a pad of Bristol board, and complain about the art
scene, in particular a Lodi gallery owner named Jeanette whom she
considered her greatest rival.

"Complete and total airhead," Carol said.

I would tidy the dining room: push papers into stacks, sharpen
her pencils, take dishes into the kitchen, and dust off the television
and the drink cart it sat on. The dust was sticky and it smeared
around the top of the television instead of coming off. Sometimes
I'd use a wet paper towel, but the grime was destined to stay on the
surface.

"You don't need to fuss with all that," Carol would say. "Your only
job is to keep me accountable to keep working."

"I just like to stay busy," I'd say.

"I can't stand women with tattoos," she'd say, turning her focus back to *Maury*.

After a few hours, she'd give me three twenty-dollar bills and a ride home. This happened every Sunday. Before too long I was very rich.

Lindsay didn't like the idea of me working for Carol. She thought it was inappropriate for me to be spending so much time with her grandma. I think she was afraid I would gossip to Carol about her, but Lindsay's drama was never that interesting to me. She had even asked Carol to fire me. But Carol was as selfish and manipulative as her granddaughter. She liked the power dynamic that was created by employing me, how it pitted me and Lindsay against each other. Lindsay would come over sometimes during my shift and be like, "Grandma, let's go for a walk, I never get to spend time with you anymore," and Carol would go, "Me and Joey are in the middle of something very important. How about you make us all some egg salad?" And Lindsay would be like, "Why don't you have the hired help do that," and Carol would say, "It's a little below Joey's pay grade, sweetheart."

For high school graduation, Lindsay's grandma Carol gave me a check for two hundred dollars. Lindsay told me if I cashed it, she'd consider it elder abuse and never speak to me again.

Then she changed her mind and said I should split the money with her fifty-fifty. We could go to the mall and buy cocktail dresses. I said that sounded great but it was too late, I had already ripped up the check per her request. I asked her if she wanted me to speak to Carol about why she had told me to destroy the check and then Carol could issue a new one?

Lindsay didn't want me to do that. To punish me she disinvited me to the graduation party her mom was throwing.

Of course I cashed the check. I wasn't an idiot.

When I got home, I had an email from Catie: *Hey girl! I'm just following up about the* Rushmore *project. I want an update on how it's going! I'm excited to see the finished product. I'd also love to see some clips that I might be able to use in my showreel! No rush, I'm just super excited!* ☺

Coming of age as an artist

Expectation: A little inner turmoil, which you make art about.

Reality: So much inner turmoil that it has found a way to multiply, becoming so massive and relentless that any art you attempt to make about your inner turmoil becomes another source that fuels it.

A text to Mom: *Jenny messaged me a while ago but now she won't respond*

Mom called. I declined Mom's call, preferring to text, then once the call was missed, I called her back guiltily.

"Hey, I'm driving to work, I didn't want to text," Mom said. She sounded panicked, possibly drunk. I wondered if it was common to show up to the hospital drunk or hungover. It was disturbing to know that medical professionals were people with lives and grievances and mental illnesses just like everyone else. Anytime I went to the hospital I couldn't help but look at the nurses and think, *I bet you steal toilet paper from work like my mom does.*

"Jenny said she's stuck in Reno," she said.

"Yeah, that's what she told me, too," I said.

"She asked me to wire her money so she can come home tonight. I honestly don't have a choice. I need her to come back, I can't afford a babysitter for Brian anymore. She's not telling me where to wire the money. How do you wire money?"

"I have no clue."

"I guess she followed some guy there. Thought she could make a bunch of money doing god knows what then come back after the weekend. Not fucking sure why she didn't think to tell me she was leaving Brian behind. Hold on I'm getting a call, it might be her."

I pulled a book about Kandinsky I had checked out from the library out of my backpack and leafed through it. I was trying to find some compositions to copy in my sketchbook drawings.

"Just a telemarketer. Okay. Well, I don't know what to say. I don't have any extra money right now, and she's acting like a bus ticket costs hundreds of dollars."

"She told me she wanted to get a hotel," I said.

"Oh, perfect," Mom said dramatically. She sighed loudly.

"She's just so fucking selfish," I said.

"Oh, stop. That doesn't help."

"She shouldn't have done this to you. Once she comes back you should kick her out of the house. She can figure out how to be an adult."

I turned to a page in my sketchbook with what looked like a one-point perspective drawing, with random shapes interrupting the perspective lines. It gave me the impression of sounds layered on top of one another. Music, car noise, people yelling.

"I don't need this from you right now, Joey," Mom said. "Seriously."

"What? She's just going to do this again if you don't stand up for yourself."

"You know what? Mind your own business. I don't know how I raised you to feel entitled to have opinions about other peoples' lives."

I scrolled up through old messages from Jenny. I wished I could scroll through our entire lifetime, back to the beginning. I would scroll back to the day I was born if I could. Lore has it Jenny was excited to be a big sister. She didn't want anyone else to have a turn holding me.

I'd like to see what she said to me in those first few weeks. What simple, gentle toddler noises she made to try to calm me.

But my phone scrolled back only five months, it wasn't even ten texts, and most of them from me to her, asking where she was only after my mom begged me to try to get a hold of her.

Seeing them all at once, my repeated *Where are you?* texts ironically displayed a subtext of keen disinterest in where she was, a bored recital of a question I was being asked to ask, and that I didn't expect an answer to.

I typed out a new message, trying to convey my feelings honestly, to get my frustration with her across, but also my love, my worry, written in my own true voice, but it came out as: *Hello? Jenny? you ever going back to Moms?*

For our final in English, we were supposed to write a series of connected poems. My first thought was that I'd make poems about *Rushmore*, about disappointing myself with my bad art ideas, about the experience of being a fucking moron, of facing the reality that I may never have a good idea ever again. I could look up the definition of *idea* and see if there was a way to interpret the word to disparage myself, as if my "ideas" didn't actually qualify as ideas, idk, depending on how the definition was worded. I could use the third person so there'd be some distance. Presupposing I had ever had an "idea" in the first place.

My mom said, "it must be nice" to struggle with something as unimportant and frivolous as a film project.

What a luxury, she meant, that appearing to be a dumbass in front of my peers was one of my most pressing concerns.

I agreed with my family that I did not deserve the opportunities I'd been given. Many of the opportunities arose by accident. Oops. It was an aggressive act of rejection toward everything I came from to accept these opportunities. It was outright violence to become interested in what the opportunities represented, to follow them, to try to build off them and make something even greater for myself, to achieve a level of greatness that no one wished for me to achieve, knowing that my family would be left behind.

It must be nice not to have to redefine *love* to accommodate the feelings you have for your family.

I closed my eyes and saw the anthropomorphic Hamburger Helper glove waving to me from an uninhabited grocery store aisle. He was always waiting for me there, I knew, eagerly anticipating my inevitable need to return to his way of life, reaching out to me from the past where I was someone else. I loved him and feared him and craved him at my lowest moments.

Each day I was bombarded by the idea that nothing mattered. Books, peers, history, school, my bank account, store clerks, my family, the internet. Everything seemed to reinforce the idea that life was a cycle of chaotic randomness to which people were desperate to attach meaning.

Within this context, preparing Hamburger Helper for myself at 3:00 a.m. was a gesture of self-love.

When I was drunk and hungry and it was too late to cook but I did it anyway because I wanted to feel good, that was a way of meaningfully existing.

And when I was holding the bowl to my chest, the warm, oily smells coating every feeling in my skull and giving them a skin, I felt taken care of despite not deserving it. It helped me understand that I was not only someone who wanted love, but also someone who could give it.

Our self-portrait film presentations were staggered, and the first two students, chosen at random when the project was assigned, were now presenting their films. This signaled that my time to work on *Rushmore* was narrowing. I had still barely started. It was time to become scared and desperate.

A girl named Alivia showed her piece first, which was a silent film depicting her trying to teach herself various circus performer acts: tightrope walking, acrobatics, and a few painful-looking but funny attempts at contortionism.

Lights came on and the class discussed physical comedy, mimes, silent films, and the comedic power of a well-timed facial expression.

Then Larissa showed her film, shot in an empty parking lot, mostly empty Walmart aisles, and some bushes behind a suburban house, with voice-over detailing the sexual abuse she had experienced as a young teenager. It was difficult to watch, and especially awkward after the comical tone of the previous film, and the disparity gave me a guilty knot in my stomach.

Lights came on, and we discussed how the voice-over itself felt predatory, a bad memory that clung to every new present moment and infected it, making it impossible to live in anything but the past.

Nobody mentioned the tension between the two films, how cruel and insane it was that people having such wildly different experiences of the world would have to sit together in a room and pretend that there was no overlap, that one kind of life could exist without the other.

Someone once told me, though I wasn't sure why they thought this, or maybe I misunderstood, or maybe it was something I made up in a dream, but anyway: When you went to sleep your brain shut down and the cells that made you who you were got put back together in a different way and in the morning you were someone else and the subconscious of your new brain had to quickly assess its surroundings and come up with some plausible story for who you were and why you were there and what you'd been through without your conscious self realizing that the subconscious mind was inventing a reality. And this happened to every person in the whole world. Every day. And that made a lot of sense given that I did not know what the fuck was going on and that every morning I was surprised that I still didn't know what the fuck to do.

I looked at my body for what felt like the first time in several weeks and was surprised that it was still there as I remembered it, that I hadn't become a formless mass with two arms sticking out, controlled remotely by a conceptual artist working through their ideas about the mundanity of human existence.

I killed a bug in the shower, then cried about it.

Afterward, I kept telling myself, *You didn't mean to kill a bug, you thought the bug was a fleck of dirt or debris,* knowing that wasn't true. I had killed the bug on purpose, knowing it had a life.

I considered dressing myself up as Jason Schwartzman. It would be easy enough. Brown fluffy wig. Mole. Eyes that seemed to have never witnessed pain.

I could reenact *Rushmore* from nothing, I thought. Screw Catie's memory. Even without storyline or dialogue, the film still had meaning to me. There was a reason, after all, that I chose it. There was a reason I hadn't watched it, despite believing that I would probably like it. Withholding things from yourself was a power. Calling something pretentious because you didn't understand it was a thrill. *Rushmore* didn't exist except in people's minds.

I decided to walk through the student galleries before going to the drawing studio. There was an anti-choice exhibit hanging in the Poundstone Gallery. People had been fucking with it, turning the canvases upside down, writing obscenities in the guest book. I wondered if it was all some kind of interactive performance piece that the artist had coordinated. It might have been an overly generous assumption, but I couldn't accept that someone would put art like that up in a place like this if they didn't want a negative reaction.

I analyzed the handwriting of some of the guest book entries, to see if it looked like they came from the same hand. I couldn't tell, but a lot of the entries were short and insult-based. There were no long, personal appeals for the artist to think differently, which I would have expected from the smug intellectuals I shared campus with.

Benji walked in as I was turning to leave.

"Hey, what's up?" he said.

"Oh, hey. Nothing. I'm headed to the drawing studio. I might go steal coffee from the painting studio first."

"Hey, would it be weird if I asked for your phone number? I had it before but I got a new phone and stuff."

"Not weird," I said. "I can give it to you."

He handed me his phone and I typed in my number, then I handed it back to him and he did some typing of his own. His curly brown hair had gotten longer and wilder. It was swept up off his forehead and tucked behind his ears, a few strands left behind, stuck on beard stubble. There was a small silver stud in his ear I never noticed before.

"I'm totally going to text you later."

"Okay."

"So get ready," Benji said.

"I'm very ready," I said, feeling sort of ready.

Benji winced, pretending to be scared at my degree of readiness.

"Don't be *too* ready," he said.

"I'll be the proper balance of ready and not ready," I said.

"It's important that you're adequately prepared for this."

"Yeah. I am. Talk to you later."

"Yes, you will," he said. "I mean, if you want."

He bumped his shoulder into the doorway as he left, but made no immediate indication that he noticed himself doing this. I watched him walk down the hall and once he was almost to the library he grabbed his shoulder and rubbed it.

Benji texted, *Can I make you dinner sometime?*

I texted, *Ok but I only eat baby seal*

He texted, *Okay so the wharf then? tmrw night?*

I texted: *Thats sea lions honey*

I texted: *tho they are tasty sometimes*

He took a long time to respond but eventually texted, *haha*. I regretted the joke about baby seals, worrying that it seemed as if I was brushing him off like all the other times I had brushed him off, or that he was disturbed I had called him *honey*, or he didn't understand that was my way of flirtatiously infantilizing him, but I didn't know how to undo any of it, or how to say yes to an actual dinner.

Once, as a teenager, I slammed the car door onto Jenny's fingers. It was an accident, but I wasn't sorry it happened. I pretended I didn't realize what I had done, and walked away from the car, toward Kmart, in a casual way that no one would walk away like if they knew they had just smashed someone's fingers in a car door. I feigned surprise when she opened the door, screaming.

"What the fuck?" I said.

"You're saying 'what the fuck' *to me*?" she said. "Fuck you!"

The night before, I had been working on a painting at the dining table. I normally never brought my paintings home from school, but I wanted to submit something to the county fair art show, and the deadline was the next day. It was a gray and blue barren landscape with a figure on one side, bent over into a sort of seated fetal position. It was supposed to be about loneliness, the acute pain of having no one. I hadn't sketched it out first, though, and the figure was too elongated and somewhat skeletal. I was trying to fill the figure out with a paint color that didn't quite match.

"Looks like a Tool video," Jenny had said. "But more stupid."

Jenny's hand was fine, nothing was broken. I told her I was sorry, gave her a side-hug, trembled a little to indicate my (false) shock, and briefly contemplated getting involved in theater. It felt natural to pretend.

Suz's parents had flown in from Los Angeles for Suz's birthday, and invited Diana and me out for birthday dinner. On the way, Suz warned me, "My parents are going to be really annoying. You don't have to answer their questions."

Diana said, "Shut up. Your parents are adorable."

"That's how they lure you in. Once they trap you in their web of charisma, they're an absolute nightmare."

"Whatever. My parents are like if *The Real Housewives of Topeka* was a thing."

"Your mom is a sweetheart, Di."

"Tell that to her six chihuahuas."

Suz saw her parents and started waving at them from across the street. Somehow I wasn't expecting them to look so different from each other. Her mom was short and stunning, wearing big gold leaf-shaped earrings and layers of colorful textured fabrics. She was probably the most beautiful woman I had ever seen in person. Her dad was tall and overweight, wearing a blue polo with a T-shirt underneath. Both of them were animatedly excited to see Suz.

"Joey, this is my dad, Paul, and my mom, Fatma," Suz said. "This is Joey. And you guys remember Diana."

"Yes, yes," Fatma said, and immediately hugged me. "Great to finally meet the famous Joey."

I could feel Suz's apologetic stare as they asked me questions. *What are you studying? What medium are you working in now? Are you going to apply to grad school?* But I wasn't annoyed. I felt encouraged by being taken seriously, by being seen as someone with artistic value. Perhaps I was being lured in. Perhaps I liked it.

"Where are you from?" Fatma said.

"Not far from here," I said. "Lodi."

"Oh, Lodi! You must know a lot about wine."

"I mean, not really. The wine scene is pretty separate from the, uh, regular-people scene."

"We love Lodi wines," Fatma said, looking dreamily at Paul.

Then they asked Diana about what she had been working on in school, and about how some project from the previous semester had turned out, and about her brother, whom they had apparently met last time they were in town.

Paul ordered sushi for the table without looking at the menu, plus miso soup and edamame and a sashimi appetizer. When the waitress left, he presented a large, heavy-looking yellow gift bag decorated with cartoon balloons and handed it to Suz. Suz rested the bag on the floor and pulled out a boxed laser printer.

"Awesome. Thank you so much," she said.

"I used up all my printing credit at the media center a month ago and I've been bitching about it to my parents," she said to me.

"You've been bitching about it to me, too," Diana said. "I thought I'd never hear the end of Suz's Great Print Credit Saga."

Suz's parents laughed.

"Oh shit, I forgot to order sake," Paul said. He gestured for the waitress to come back and ordered hot sake for all of us.

"I have a gift for you in our fridge," Diana said.

"I have a gift for you at home," I said, lying.

I took the tiniest sip possible, unsure if the liquid in the cup was supposed to last as long as a regular drink or be taken more like a shot. Suz laughed, thinking I was joking.

Suz caught her parents up on the last few weeks in her life, including boastful details I would never have given to my own family, such as, "My sculpture professor invited me to take his grad-level class next semester," and, "I watched this great Kara Walker lecture I keep meaning to forward to you."

I felt a small ball of anger building in my chest. I tried to avoid analyzing the feeling, sensing it would probably put me in a bad mood. *People have parents like this*, I thought. *People grow up with parents that have conversations with them.* I drank what was left in my sake cup and Paul quickly gave me a refill.

"Your mom and I were thinking you and Joey and Diana might like to spend next winter break at our house in Tahoe," Paul said. "We aren't going to be able to go this year since we'll be in London."

"Oh my god. Yes," Diana said. "I've always wanted to see Tahoe. Oh my god."

I had never skied, nor seen Tahoe, even though Tahoe was only two hours away from Lodi. It had never even occurred to me as a possibility. It was as impossibly far away as Portugal or Venice or the International Space Station.

"Haven't you?" Fatma said. "You'd love it, Diana. I hope you'll go."

"We're in," Diana said. "If Suz and Joey don't want to go, they can just suck it up for my sake."

"I've never been, either," I said. "Sounds cool."

"I hate skiing," Suz said, groaning. "But Tahoe is great. It will be a blast."

"Great!" Paul said. "We'll set it all up. We can rent a car for you guys or reserve plane tickets if you'd prefer. And we'll have someone out to spruce the place up and stock it with groceries before you arrive."

Our food arrived, and I mimicked the way others were eating, putting one piece of sushi on their plate at a time and eating it before taking another. On the final day of Painting class of my first semester at school, our professor had taken us all out to sushi. I'd ordered the Dragon Roll at random, having no experience with sushi and since the menu was lacking photos of the food. The Dragon Roll came and my whole life collapsed into its eight pieces. I knew we were receiving some kind of end-of-class inspirational lecture, but I heard nothing. I was struggling to use chopsticks, but I felt no shame or insecurity. That meal had been a beautiful black hole from which I'd emerged all at once looking down at my plate, which had been licked clean.

I tried to stay conscious for this meal. Be more chill about things. I ate pieces slowly, looked around at my surroundings while I chewed, and tried to stay involved in the conversation. I drank from my constantly refilled sake cup. I ate a piece of white fish that might've changed my life if I let it, but I did not. I chewed and swallowed.

"I love your sweater," Fatma said, caressing my baggy sleeve.

"Thanks, it's vintage," I said. "I wear it a lot because I like to confuse people as to whether or not I'm poor, because I think it gives the impression that I don't care about class signifiers, which I think makes me seem rich."

Suz laughed in a way that made me think I might be embarrassing her. She was making an expression in Diana's direction that I couldn't decipher. Maybe you weren't supposed to talk about being poor in front of rich people.

"It's gorgeous," Fatma said. I couldn't tell if the sound in the restaurant suddenly changed or if I was having a moment of tinnitus.

"Well, are you almost ready for Detroit?" Paul said.

"Yeah," Suz said. She looked at me and then looked away.

"Detroit?" I said. "Are you visiting your cousin?"

"No," Suz said quietly. "I got that residency I applied for. They accepted me a couple weeks ago."

"Oh," I said. "I didn't know about that."

I noticed I was too big for my chair. Was it a child's chair? I twisted around to look at it, but it appeared to be the same size as all the other chairs.

Fatma started listing Detroit galleries that Suz needed to check out while she was there, the names of gallery owners that Suz should make a point to meet. I imagined packing up my apartment alone, saying goodbye to no one, and leaving San Francisco forever as though I had never been here at all.

I ate more spicy tuna and held back tears.

It's funny that
"Starving artist"
is a common expression
when almost every
artist I've known
leaves pieces of
uneaten food behind
when they go out
to sushi.

"Why didn't you tell me you got that residency?" I said on our walk back to Suz and Diana's apartment. Diana had hung back behind us to answer a phone call from her own mother.

"I told you," she said.

"No, you didn't mention it." The words came out of my mouth a little more stiffly than I had intended, like we were fighting.

Congratulations, I could have said, if I were another kind of person. Or, *That's such a cool opportunity for you.* Instead, I kept my eyes fixed at a condo building being assembled in the distance.

You don't know that's a condo, my inner monologue said. *You don't even know what a condo is. Define* condo. *You can't.*

"Of course I'm happy for you that you get to do this," I said. I could feel myself beginning to cry. *A condo is a fancy apartment,* I thought angrily, trying to distract myself. A tear formed in my right eye anyway, and I wiped it roughly, trying to pass the gesture off like I was removing a piece of debris that had been bothering me for some time.

"Oh my god. You're being dramatic," Suz said.

"I just wish you had told me," I said. "It makes me feel stupid that you would hide something like that from me."

"I know. I'm sorry. I don't know why I didn't tell you. I thought you'd be upset that I was going to be gone all summer."

Another tear fell unexpectedly from my other eye, and then I was fully crying. We hugged. I could see she felt sorry for me. I had turned her good news into a sad moment centered around myself.

Hm, why don't more people want to be your friend?

I texted Lindsay. It wasn't the most dignified thing to do. We hadn't spoken since we ran into each other at Kmart a week before I left for San Francisco. I had been buying toothpaste and a new toothbrush and feeling nostalgic for all the times I had walked through Kmart. Would I ever be that young again? I turned the corner by the Ziploc bags and there was Lindsay, carrying a basket with white sandwich bread, strawberry jelly, and strawberry Pop-Tarts, staples of a Kmart run for Carol. I hadn't seen her since she had disinvited me from her graduation party. It was usually me who had to come crawling back to her after a fight, apologizing and asking to be forgiven for having my own agency. But I thought, *I'm leaving, so what's the point? Let her be mad forever.*

"You're really moving to San Francisco?" she had said.

"Yep." I showed her the toothbrush in my cart like it indicated the beginning of a life change.

"I honestly thought you'd chicken out."

"Don't be a bitch," I'd said. But I had wondered, too, if I would chicken out. Part of me was still wondering.

I miss you, I texted. *How are you doing?*

I was nostalgic for a friendship that made me feel like shit. I missed the consistency of feeling like shit in the same specific way all the time.

Writing out the script for my *Rushmore* remake, I realized I had very little information regarding the visual details of the film.

I remembered, with a suddenness that made my cheeks flush and drove my heartbeat up, that this film project was meant to be a self-portrait. I hadn't been thinking about that aspect of the project. And just what was I unintentionally revealing about myself here? That I thought I could remake a film I hadn't seen into a story about myself because I believed everything was, on a deeper level, about me? That my lack of understanding of some popular cultural touchstone was interesting to other people?

I could've studied psychology, but I preferred having homework that was impossible to do wrong, or even right.

I considered texting Catie to get more details, but it had been a long time since I talked to her. Would she even remember me? Had I carved out enough of her brain space to store details about my insanely stupid art project that she would be able to recall it? Did she remember the hours she spent with me in an empty classroom, having a conversation about a movie only one of us had seen led by the person who hadn't seen it?

Catie, please come over and do my homework for me, I thought mockingly.

I read the couple of lines of text I had written weeks before, each word less engaging than the last, ending with my blinking cursor. I wished I could grab the text and crumple it in my hand, like in movies where a writer is frustrated. I wished life was more like movies, where bad art simply existed as a punchline and did not need to be painstakingly created.

A Short Film by My Inner Monologue

Me: Hi! I'm Joey, and I'm cultivating a relationship with art in an attempt to alienate myself from everyone around me.

Image of me pulling a large and disgusting wad of something out of the bathroom drain.

Pull back to show me photographing a clump of hair and drain gunk.

Me: And it's working.

Close up of my reflection in the mirror as I wink.

My inner monologue, waking me up in the middle of the night: *If you're an artist, why is making art so difficult and monotonous? If you're an artist, why the bad attitude toward every part of the process?*

Hey, Lindsay texted fourteen hours later. I saw the text come in, and waited for a follow-up, a response to one or both points in my text. I got up from my bed and got a glass of water from the kitchen and when I came back there was still no follow-up text. I opened my laptop and checked my email and then looked at my phone again, even though I would have heard the sound of the text notification if I had gotten one. I took a shower, making a point to use every hair and body product I had, and even half-heartedly shaved one of my legs. When I was finished, I blow-dried my hair, combed it, moisturized, then returned to my phone to see no new messages.

This was how it was with Lindsay. She could sense when she was needed, and liked to make me beg.

Things are falling apart here, Lindsay likely expected me to text. *You were right about living in the city being too much for me. I should have gotten a job in the wine industry, like you. I think about this every day as I struggle to make art, hanging my head before my easel in solemn regret. Now it is too late. You are a symbol of all I have foolishly squandered.*

What did I need her for anyway? I had texted her in a moment of self-pity in which I needed to make myself feel worse as a reminder that many things were shitty, not just whatever shitty thing I was currently dealing with. It was done. I felt worse. Mission accomplished. There was no real need to carry on with this.

How many times had Suz and I hung out after she knew she'd gotten the residency? Perhaps I was being too possessive of Suz. She wanted to do things without my input, as was her right. I was just one of her many equally unimportant friends. She was pulling away. I realized I should have cried in the shower. If I cried now, my face would get puffy.

I didn't text Lindsay again.

I drew from a photo of Suz I had saved on my computer. It wasn't recommended to draw from photos for Drawing II. "We're not drawing what we see, we're drawing what it feels like to see it," Professor Long often said. But I was many drawings behind and didn't feel like going into public to secretly draw strangers. I had taken the photo months ago in her apartment. In the photo she is standing up, thrusting her pelvis forward, arms pumping in the air, her teeth bared.

"Yeah, yeah, gimme summa that," Suz had said, though I can't remember what about. But I remember laughing as I took these photos, tears streaming down my face.

I tried to draw what it felt like to look at the photo. Playfulness, I guess, or a slight nostalgia for that day being gone forever, the passage of time or whatever. I drew one long, easy C to create the shape of her back and bent legs. Some oval shapes on top of the line to indicate her firm legs planted on the ground. For hands I made curly marks without lifting my pen from the paper. I wanted my drawing to look effortless, like I felt that day, but it was not looking much like a person so far. I added a head and a few scribbly lines for a face. A thick dark block of hair. I flipped to a new page to try again.

Working from the same photo, I tried to be more slow and specific with my lines. More small shapes instead of long unbroken lines, lots of erasing, starting again even closer with more details.

I looked through some of the other photos from that day, and found one with Diana in the background, slouching in the shadows of their breakfast nook, one arm over her stomach, the other hand holding her chin. I hadn't remembered her being there with us that day, and she was in only a couple of the photos, as if she sat down for only a few moments and then decided it wasn't where she wanted to be. I felt sorry that I hadn't seen her, or that I had seen her and didn't think to include her. I used the side of a charcoal pencil to shade the page over where I had been trying to draw Suz. I used my eraser to make the shapes of Diana's body that wasn't in shadow, and then made the deep shadow areas darker. There weren't many details to add, since she was in the background of a digital photo and pretty blurry and out of focus, but I added a few where I could see them, in the creases of her arms, at her jawline where light met dark, two small spots to indicate an eyelid and the ridge of her nose.

She looked sort of ghostly, not in a dead way but like we weren't meant to see her, revealing a sadness I had never noticed before.

We had planned to hang out and give each other feedback on some in-progress work, but by the time I showed up at her apartment, Suz had changed her mind and wanted to go to a party she'd been invited to earlier in the day.

"I don't know," I said. "I have a lot to do."

"Okay, well I'm gonna go. This art collector that I really want to meet is supposed to be there. You're more than welcome to join me."

She took off her overalls and put on black-and-white tie-dye jeans. She left on the yellow crop top she'd been wearing all day and swept her hair up into a quick bun. She made beauty look effortless. I considered what my own clothes said about me. A thin striped button-up shirt I'd gotten from Kmart sophomore year of high school and some faded green chinos, also from high school. In the context of a fancy art party, I would look like a street urchin Suz was ironically friends with.

Suz, reading my mind, threw me a long blue velvet coat from her closet, something I had never seen before.

"That will look dope with those green pants," she said.

Part of me felt embarrassed for needing to be dressed to go out, but another part of me felt like going out in a jacket this cool could actually change my life.

I recognized everyone at the party, or everyone looked like someone I'd seen before, or they were all following the same style format as other people I'd seen, or I didn't recognize faces well. Not that it mattered, since I didn't plan on talking much to anybody unless someone approached me and asked me what fast food chicken sandwich I thought was the best and five reasons why. That was the only question I was ever truly ready for. But no one ever asked me that. No one cared. No one wanted to know. It wasn't the kind of thing people found interesting. Or everyone already had an opinion, and their opinion was that chicken sandwiches weren't interesting to talk about with people you were just meeting. Or had already met. Recognized, anyway. Or nothing was real and the simulation was running out of original people to populate parties.

"My muse," a girl in overalls said to Suz, hugging her, their cigarette smoke entangling. I stood there for a few minutes waiting for someone to claim me as their muse, then realized everyone had shifted about two feet away from me and had formed a circle without me, someone in the circle saying *Duchamp* loud enough for me to know I had no place within it.

Hey, what if your life wasn't fake and annoying and you were getting a degree in a subject you could participate in a conversation about? my inner monologue said.

I walked over to a wall I thought I could lean against but when I got over to it there was a white canvas hanging up on it. Not painted white, just raw stretched canvas, with some possibly intentional scratch marks on it. I would never have thought to hang this up on the wall.

Hello? I said what if your life wasn't fake and annoying.

I walked around the apartment, found an opened bottle of wine on the kitchen counter, and then made a series of motions that would have looked weird if someone were watching me but wouldn't look weird at all if I was in everyone's peripheral vision, which I suspected I was, because no one cared that I was there; the series of motions consisting of picking the bottle up to look at the label, moving as if I were going to set the bottle back down on the counter but instead putting it down by my hip, below counter level where no one could see it, then a few moments later moving my body to look like I had dropped something on the floor and needed to bend down below counter level to pick it up, and then, instead of bending back up, sitting down and drinking from the bottle until it was empty.

I stood back up and made eye contact with Suz from across the room, and she gave me a look that seemed to say they were about to start debating chicken and I should come join them, but I knew they wouldn't. It was always *Duchamp this*, and *de Stijl that*, and *Damien Hirst's urine is on display at the MOMA and tickets are only four hundred dollars.*

Emboldened by the wine in my system, I tried to find more unattended, unfinished bottles. I found two unopened beer bottles in the fridge. I opened both and then wove through the party in a manner I thought would suggest the confidence of someone retrieving two beers for themselves and a friend, then found a bathroom and locked myself inside of it. I drank the first beer casually, then someone jiggled the doorknob to the bathroom and I said, "hold on," and then drank the second beer quickly. I put both empty bottles in the bathroom trash and then left, finding no one waiting for the bathroom.

I turned back toward the main room where people were hanging out and saw Benji, standing alone near the white canvas. I had never been so happy to see a fellow fucking idiot in my entire idiot life.

"Hi!" I said.

"Oh, hey," he said. "I wasn't expecting to see you here."

"Do you normally come to these parties?" I said, not knowing what other parties I was referring to.

"Sometimes," he said, probably not knowing what I meant either. Grinning excitedly, he handed me a half-full bottle of whiskey and I drank from it. I felt relieved that I had someone to stand next to. I thought I sensed him smiling and I covertly looked over at him and confirmed he was smiling, his thick lashes obscuring his eyes completely.

We sat underneath the white canvas and continued drinking, passing the bottle back and forth. When the bottle was done he took a second bottle out of his backpack.

"I might drop out and be a coder," he said.

"Not gonna talk you out of that," I said.

Our bodies slumped onto the floor until we were almost laying down. I bragged about not having to share a refrigerator with roommates. I told him that when I thought about Lodi it felt like I was thinking about a place thousands of miles away. I told him I played *FarmVille*.

"The most fucked-up thing about rape and torture scenes in movies isn't the rape and torture, it's that people find that stuff entertaining to watch," he said.

At some point we started holding hands. At some point we kissed. At some point Suz came over and asked me if I wanted water and I said, "Yes, baby, yes." At some point Benji stood up to demonstrate a football play he was describing to me and somehow fell onto his back, ripping a large chunk of his thumbnail off and bleeding onto the white canvas, which had fallen onto the floor.

"What the fuck is wrong with you?" someone said. They grabbed Benji and lifted him up to a standing position. I thought I was sitting down and tried to stand up but I was already standing so I fell.

"Don't hit him," I said, somehow falling again.

"No one is hitting anyone," someone said.

People yelled at Benji to leave and though no one yelled at me to leave I left with him anyway. We stumbled to his apartment, took off our clothes, and fell asleep kissing.

Rushmore (2011 Joelle Berry remake)

Bill Murray invited me to have lunch at a burger shop a few blocks from campus that sold burgers without cheese for twelve dollars or with cheese for fifteen dollars and curly fries for eight dollars. It had been a while since we hung out, and I felt sort of guilty about it. Bill Murray wasn't bothered that we hadn't been hanging out much lately. I believed this was indicative of the minuscule, barely perceptible energy I added to his life.

Part of why I had pulled away was that whenever we hung out, Bill Murray always wanted to get a bite or go to a play or visit the museums. Always something that cost money, which didn't feel like a big deal my first semester of college, when my student loan was first issued and I had a part-time work-study position in the library. I thought I would always have money back then, that spending twenty dollars on seeing a play was what the money was supposed to be paying for anyway.

I decided I would go to the burger shop and not get anything, but then I decided to get curly fries at the last minute because suddenly my personal philosophy was that sometimes it's okay to spend money recklessly if it makes you feel like you have a place in this lonely, fleeting existence (I smelled the fries), but Bill Murray forgot his wallet and didn't notice until after he placed his order, so I ended up spending thirty-six dollars.

Bill Murray, sitting down in a booth: Do you *get* futurism?

I thought of *Dynamism of a Dog on a Leash*, which was the only "futurism" piece I could immediately call to mind. People were always using *Dynamism of a Dog on a Leash* as the prime example of Futurism, as if they were all working from the same textbook, that art history was something with set parameters and themes and set ways of thinking about it all. I also didn't believe the dog could have been walking as fast as the painting made it look.

Me (Jason Schwartzman): It's about movement, right?

Bill Murray started saying strings of words: "perspective," "capture," "glimpse," and "curvature." I nodded patiently, lovingly, knowing he was considering majoring in Art History and wanting to support that decision even if I didn't understand it.

The waiter brought my curly fries and Bill Murray's hot dog and shoestring fries and vanilla milkshake and then asked if there was anything else we needed. I asked for ranch dressing.

Bill Murray, laughing louder and more jubilantly than seemed warranted: Have you been here before? You're going to have to be more specific.

Waiter: We have classic ranch. Buffalo ranch. Greek yogurt ranch. Cajun ranch. Balsamic ranch. Vegan ranch.

Me: Cajun ranch, I guess.

Bill Murray, winking at the waiter: We'll take Greek yogurt ranch, too.

Any word from Jenny? I texted my mom. *Is she coming home?*

It was one in the morning and I was walking home from another party. Suz had accompanied me there but left early to finish her film project. I meant to finish my beer and leave shortly after her, but then people started reading poetry near the door and I would have had to pass in front of them to leave, so I stayed and zoned out until they finished at 12:30 a.m.

Walking down Van Ness, I scrolled back through my messages to remember the date Jenny had first disappeared. It had been thirty-five days.

My stomach dropped with the horrific realization that fast-food places wouldn't be open to foot traffic at this hour. I had nothing at home except peanut butter and a jar of marinara.

I imagined Jenny's dead body splayed across an intersection. Not bloody or broken, but recognizably dead. I waited for my stomach to drop again but it did not.

I wondered what it would be like to be the center of my own universe, for my thoughts to orbit around my own needs and desires the way I had always been accused of, without being constantly magnetically drawn back to some other person with problems that were supposedly bigger and more important than mine.

Worrying about someone doesn't count if you resent them for making you worry.

I was hungry, and thought of texting Benji, asking him to come over, asking him to stop at Taco Bell in his car on the way over, get me a seven-layer burrito and nachos and a Baja Blast.

I texted Benji: *Want to come over and draw?*

No i dont no, my mom texted. It was now 1:23 a.m.

Benji texted: *Yeah, dude!*

I called my mom.

"Hello?" my mom said.

"Hi. I didn't expect you to be awake. I'm just walking home."

"Oh, yeah. I got out of bed because I forgot to feed Thomas and the son of a bitch wouldn't stop meowing at me and clawing my pillow. Then I got up and saw that he had ralphed all over the kitchen floor. Now I'm cleaning that all up, so."

"Oh."

"So yeah, nothing new from Jenny. My coworker Janelle's daughter Kasey is going to watch Brian tomorrow. I've never met her but Janelle said she's reliable and I don't really have a choice, I have to go to work."

"Okay. Well, I'm sure everything will be fine. I'm glad you found someone to watch him."

"All right. Yeah. I'm going to go back to bed."

"Okay," I said. "I love you."

The word was nonspecific, and I appreciated that. I didn't have to psychoanalyze myself to determine the specifics of my feelings because there was a word that encompassed all the comfort and all the pain at once.

"Bye. Love you."

Benji brought over a joint to share with me. I had forgotten to ask him about Taco Bell, but he had come over on his skateboard anyway. I wasn't supposed to smoke in my apartment, but it was too cold to stand outside so I opened the window and we sat near it. I had David Bowie playing from my laptop, something I put on when I had guests over not because I particularly liked the music but because I believed it was something no one could complain about. I ate a spoonful of peanut butter and waited for a drug-induced miracle to occur and help me move forward with the *Rushmore* thing.

"It would be so sick to design shoes, man," Benji said. "It's my fucking dream."

"Oh cool. I love . . . shoes," I said.

"That's what's so sick. They're like an everyday utilitarian item that everyone needs. But also art. It's both."

I looked at his sketchbook. Benji had drawn the words *Fuck All* in graffiti letters in his sketchbook and was now outlining the words with a thick black stroke.

I underlined the title of my notes. <u>*Rushmore.*</u> I underlined it again.

"And like, people would just be walking around with your art on their feet. Everywhere they go. Into Target. To the dentist. To the fucking airport, man. To Europe and shit."

I wanted to write down what he said so that I could remember it later and make fun of him with Suz, but I didn't want him to see and be insulted.

"It would be a lot of . . . exposure," I said.

Benji laughed.

"Fucking exactly," he said.

well it happened.

I had sex with
someone who
thinks shoes are
cool.

Suz presented her self-portrait project for Experimental Film. It was composed of the rich, colorful eighties film of Fatma in the garden, cut up and collaged back together to form a loose narrative about a sexual awakening.

"They're getting ready to bloom," Fatma says, her face close to a row of emerging bulbs, a few stray hairs caught in her thick eyelashes, batting up and down. The voice echoes for a few seconds, like, *bloom bloom bloom bloom*. It cuts to Fatma's back as she steps out of frame, revealing a row of tulips, then cuts to Fatma sitting on a bench beneath two fruiting apple trees. The film runs for a couple of minutes as she sits there, uneasy. There are a few frames of her picking flowers, then a child is there picking flowers with her.

"Suz, don't pick those ones," Fatma says to the child, then she rushes over and redirects her to a different kind of flower. "Those aren't for picking."

The film follows a tiny Suz in a blunt black bob as she picks an assortment of flowers, sometimes being redirected by her mother. Subtitles appear that read THOSE AREN'T FOR PICKING every time her mother leads her away from something she is picking.

The class bubbled with excitement. What a gorgeous meditation, people commented, on the meaning of womanhood, the ease and lightness women feel they need to manufacture in order to appear feminine, the arbitrary rules that are given to them. It was also, the class said, a comment on the pressures of being a daughter living up to the expectations of her mother. The garden was beautiful and reminded one of the transience of youth, particularly the way femininity is valued only during youth.

Suz looked at me for support. It was the kind of feedback Suz dreaded. Too positive. Too shallow. Not rooted in enough art history or theory. But I didn't know what she wanted me to say.

"Inspired work," Herrera said. "What an achievement."

After class, Suz asked if I wanted to go get sushi, but I said I needed to go home and work on *Rushmore*. I told her I'd walk with her though, since the restaurant was on the way to my apartment. She left her things in one of the senior painting studios, which the senior shared with Suz for no apparent reason, as a favor to Suz out of the goodness of their heart, I guessed.

I carried my big sketch board in my right arm as we walked down the quiet part of Sixteenth, where the buses whoosh past you, unhesitant. There were few businesses here, and therefore few pedestrians. We walked abreast unselfconsciously, taking up the whole sidewalk, going blocks without smelling someone else's personal odors.

"I hooked up with Benji last night," I said.

"Oh, wow," Suz said, effectively disguising her judgment and disgust. "How was it?"

"It was cool and fine but today I saw him in the main hall and he was like, *what are you doing after class, what about later tonight, here's a black-and-white photo of a gumball machine I want you to have.*"

"Wow, he must be really into you," she said.

"Weird," I said.

Suz was silent for a minute, then sighed loudly.

"What?" I said.

"Oh. I was just disappointed by critique today. No matter what I make, people always think it's about womanhood or sexism. It feels like people can't see beyond my identity, or can't imagine me having ideas that aren't wrapped up in my gender. It's frustrating."

"Yeah, it's hard," I said, not fully understanding what I was agreeing with. She had received lots of feedback, all of it positive. I liked receiving positive feedback of my work, even if the response wasn't exactly what I'd intended. It made me feel like I was going in the right direction when I often had no idea what direction I was going in at all.

"Like, because I am a woman my work must be about those things and nothing else, nothing bigger. I don't even agree with the assumption that my art needs to be *about* anything."

"Right," I said. The assignment had been a self-portrait, after all. But maybe my understanding of self-portrait was too limited. I thought about a film project one of our classmates made, in which he had filmed himself reading a long poem while hanging upside down on some kind of gym equipment bar. Our class hadn't discussed his maleness, his privileged position within a lineage of straight white dudes, or anything about his personal feelings about any of this. We had talked about the content of the poem, which was about soldiers, and what it meant that he was hanging upside down reading such a thing. The class had decided it was a commentary on isolation.

"Anyway," she said, and didn't say anything else.

Suz and I parted, and I walked the remaining few blocks to my apartment alone among the crowd.

I had to wake up early and take the BART and then a bus to Berkeley to arrive at a generic office building by 9:00 a.m. Once there, I sat in a waiting room for an hour, reading a magazine about weight loss. Then a woman who smelled like Victoria's Secret Love Spell ushered me into another room, put goo on various points of my scalp, then put a latex hat over my head, then snapped in little wires. I liked the sensation of being touched.

I was led to a dark room with a big screen and left alone there. It was a "neuromarketing study" but I couldn't figure out what they were attempting to sell. The woman, now in a different room and talking to me over an intercom, told me to watch a screen when numbers and images floated in and out of view, and when certain numbers appeared to click a button on a remote as soon as I could. First I was told to click the button when I saw "4," then "9." Then I was told to click the button if I saw a frog. The room was warm and I had to try hard not to fall asleep and succeeded. They gave me a check for one hundred dollars and I took the bus to school, scalp still full of greasy goo.

"Freddie and I had a *talk* last night," Suz said.

"Oh, god. How did that go?"

"He told me he doesn't want me to be his girlfriend because he thinks it will cause him to lose his focus on his art."

"Why wouldn't he wait to see if that was actually a problem?"

"I think he just wants to keep his options open."

"Okay. Wow. Is he seeing other girls?"

"Probably," she said, folding over the table to cradle her head in her arms. "I don't know. I don't know."

It felt weird to see this vulnerability in Suz. Didn't she know she was much more interesting and smart and ambitious and beautiful than Freddie (or me or Diana or anyone else in her life)? The fact that Freddie couldn't see that only reflected poorly on Freddie. If Freddie ever developed sentience, rejecting Suz was the kind of fatal error he'd look back on someday when he tried to pinpoint where his life went tragically wrong. That Suz could read his sad misjudgment as reflective of her value made me wonder what cruel power our sex organs had over us. What chance did anyone have if even the most brilliant among us could be brought down so easily by someone so petulant (this low opinion including the benefit of the doubt I had given him because of Suz's interest)?

"Outside the context of art school, Freddie is just some dumpy bro who makes ambient soundscapes no one will ever listen to. He'll end up an accountant who hates himself and live in the suburbs married to some woman who will never not have baby bangs. He's a moron."

"Wow, dude. Someone's got opinions."

I realized I had gone too far. They hadn't broken it off completely, and now it was known that I didn't like him. She told me she had to go, that she was working on a sculpture and had to check the progress of some drying plaster.

Later she texted: *ur a good friend <3*

I typed: *You are* and then locked my phone without sending the text.

"Oh look, that's terrible," the woman in *The Conversation* says.

"He's not hurting anyone," the man she is with says.

"Neither are we," she says. "Oh god. Every time I see one of those old guys I always think the same thing."

"What do you think?"

"I always think that he was once somebody's baby boy. I do, I think he was once somebody's baby boy. And he had a mother and a father who loved him. And now, there he is, half dead on a park bench. And where are his mother or his father or all his uncles now?"

But that was me. I was the selfish invisible family member living alone in her warm apartment. I was the person who didn't want to invite chaos into her immediate surroundings, who wanted to spend time mostly with people who didn't outwardly resent her, who had convinced herself that her own emotional well-being was more important than someone else's physical well-being, and who believed that luck was only one part of the complicated equation that put her in a better position than others.

I was the shithead the woman in *The Conversation* always wondered about.

I woke up in the middle of the night having a panic attack because in my dream I realized I didn't know what love was supposed to feel like.

I found my phone and texted my mom, *How are you?* and waited a few minutes, holding my phone to my stomach hoping it would vibrate against whatever was aching inside me, before realizing it was 4:00 a.m. and my mom was unlikely to answer before 7 or 8. I threw my phone onto the floor and turned over in my bed.

My blankets felt dirty. They had that slick feeling fabric gets when you lay your face on it every night for months. I couldn't remember ever taking a blanket downstairs to the laundry room to wash it. I couldn't recall a specific memory of doing laundry from any time in my life.

What's a word that means "love" but makes you sound like a fucking asshole when you use it?

Text to Suz: *Hey I was in a weird mood yesterday when we talked and I took your last text as satire and saw our friendship as a massive endeavor to expose each other's gross and sad willingness to performatively pretend friendship for an audience of just each other, and this perspective hurt my feelings so that's why I didn't respond sorry wyd*

Suz: *lol it's chill. destroy the patriarchy w me tonight at my place?*

Then: *drinks on the roof at 8pm whoop whoop*

Me: *I'll be there!*

Suz didn't answer her door. I checked our text messages to make sure I hadn't imagined being invited over. No, it was there in a gray speech bubble, dated an hour prior: *drinks on the roof at 8pm whoop whoop.*

I called her.

"Oh, sorry, I didn't hear the bell, I guess. We're on the roof. I'll come get you," she said.

We. Freddie was here, too, then. I felt my mood change into something dark and fuzzy.

But when Suz and I got to the roof, I saw that it wasn't Freddie there, but Herta and another girl, both of them holding cigarettes and cans of sparkling water, their feet up on the metal plant stand Suz and I had found in the street months earlier.

We.

"You know Herta," Suz said, and Herta smiled in a way I took to mean she did not recognize me.

"And this is Charlene."

Charlene extended a hand to me and I shook it weakly. Her black hair was greasy and tangled. Her face had a lopsidedness to it that was sort of ugly, but also made me want to be ugly in that same specific, lopsided way.

"She owns that space in Noe Valley I was telling you about, Common Forms," Suz said.

"Oh, that's awesome," I said. "I love . . ." I tried to remember what Suz had told me about it but couldn't recall anything. I kept thinking of this other store we sometimes went to, that sold thin magazines about lamps for thirty dollars an issue, small potted succulents, and obscure vintage records in pristine condition. Once I went in there and got a pen dirty with some peanut butter that was on my finger. The pen was made out of some kind of velvety rubber material and I couldn't rub the peanut butter off so I turned the pen around on the table so the peanut butter was on the underside. " . . . spaces," I finally said.

"Thanks," Charlene said. "I'm going to try to convince Suz to be part of this group show I'm putting together."

"What! I would love to," Suz said. "Joey's in the Painting/Drawing department," Suz said. Apparently the major I was considering leaving was the most notable thing about me. Herta started rolling a joint.

"That's awesome," Charlene said to me, looking overly, patronizingly, interested. I felt like a child.

Suz, Herta, and Charlene seemed to return to a conversation they were previously having about something called Wunderkinetic and the Marxist arguments against it. I listened to parts of their conversation and wondered why, even after two years of hearing about Marxism and periodically looking it up, my brain could not hold on to its meaning.

I wanted a can of sparkling water but I didn't want to interrupt the flow of the conversation. The conversation moved to Henry Darger and then Christianity and then the urgent need to travel to Switzerland. I had nothing to contribute at any point. I watched them, invisible. Herta leaned too far into Charlene's personal space and nodded and laughed enthusiastically, looking desperate for Charlene's approval.

"Oh, that reminds me. I got you this." Charlene took a small handmade book out of her bag and handed it to Suz. "It's Laura Owens."

"Ohhh, awesome."

"I bought it for myself, but it kept making me think of you, so I thought you should have it. She works a lot with the idea of how her pieces interact with space."

You should say, "I love spaces" again, my inner monologue said.

"Thanks. Yeah. I love her," Suz said.

I took my phone out of my backpack and emailed myself random bits of nonsense to seem busy:

What is it called when you know you won't change your mind about something but you keep retracing all the thoughts that led you to that particular mindset, looking for holes in your own assessment, hoping to be wrong?

I want to be wrong about everything.

What's it going to take to become someone who doesn't look up synonyms for "interesting" whenever I try to write about something that interests me?

"I need to introduce you both to my friend Rebecca," Charlene said, referring to Suz and Herta, like I was not there at all, or like I was there but only eavesdropping. I thought of how Gene Hackman in

The Conversation was obsessed with the idea that he had a responsibility to the people he had been surveilling, as if he was an important part of their lives rather than a person who was privy to a single conversation they had had together in presumed privacy. Maybe I, too, was reading too much into my own existence. I looked at Suz to see if she was going to acknowledge the fact that I had been left out of Charlene's invitation, but Suz didn't seem to register the slight.

"She represents all these cool young female artists," Charlene said. "She's insanely cool. She knows everybody. She's going to love you guys."

I felt the vibration of my phone receiving a text, and flipped it open to look at it. It was from an unknown number and read, *CONGTRAS your are a WINNER get your mas$sive $1000 prize go to xxbestbuy .com/4h9pmlvp.php.*

Suz was staring at me when I looked up from my phone. She bobbed her head slightly and raised her eyebrows, trying to communicate with me that I should insert myself into the conversation, that my silence was making me invisible, that I was only hurting myself by not figuring out how to hang out properly. Instead, I replied to the unknown number, *I encourage you to rotisserie your own fucking dick and then choke on it.*

Some things I discovered about Charlene from listening to Charlene talk about herself:

Charlene's mom was an activist and journalist, currently traveling in India.

When Charlene was ten, her family went to Africa for a month for vacation and they took Charlene's art tutor with them.

Charlene had a tattoo of a Kewpie mayo bottle.

Charlene was considering hiring a social media intern.

Charlene knew what Marxism was.

There was a lull in the conversation, so I made a point to speak. I said, "Isn't it funny how when you're young and just deciding that you want to be an artist, it feels simple, that you can show up to art school like, *I want to paint!* And you think your drive to create will be enough to make you an artist? But then in the real world artistic success is all about connections and *who do you know* and *do you have representation?* It's completely the opposite of what you expect when you're young."

Everyone was quiet and I looked down at my hands, hoping that I had just had a very realistic hallucination and did not actually say any of that.

Suz said, "Well, connections are important. But that doesn't mean talent and determination are any less important. You still have to show up and do the work."

"Right," Herta said. "And being socially engaged doesn't make you fake."

"No, I'm not saying that," I said. Of course they would take offense to the idea that success was dependent on superficial relationships, like the ones they were trying to forge with each other to further their own careers.

"People think of *connections* as such a dirty word," Charlene said. "But it's pretty hard to get anywhere if you're working in a vacuum. Artists need people to come look at their work, and think about it, and talk about it."

I nodded heartily as though my mind had been changed by this brand-new information, and the conversation turned back to the topic of this woman Rebecca, who would be at some show later this week if everyone wanted to come meet her.

"She'll be there Friday, and it's VIP only that day, but I can get you guys on the list," Charlene said. "There will be bands and stuff, too," Charlene said. "Landon Grace will play a set."

"Oh," I said, perking up at the opportunity to contribute something. "I saw Landon Grace a few weeks ago at the old furniture store. It made me feel sad and weird. I had this overwhelming sense of wanting someone to love him but also the feeling that no one ever would."

"Who is this?" Herta said. "I think I missed something."

Charlene was looking at Suz and Suz was smiling back at her in a way I couldn't interpret, so I said, "This musician? I guess? Or performance artist of some kind? Who plays sad weird music that makes the audience want to commit suicide."

"My little brother," Charlene said.

The first time I talked to Suz she asked me to come over and watch *The Conversation* with her. She acted as though we knew each other from somewhere else, had shared history that made us familiar with one another when there was no such history at all. I had spent the majority of my life without her, with no idea she existed. I could have easily spent the rest of my life not knowing her. But then she was there, and I felt relieved, like I had been waiting for her the whole time.

She had sculptural objects on shelves in her bedroom that served no purpose other than being good to look at. Her apartment had color palettes that shifted from room to room but still felt cohesive, like a magazine about interior design. She had jackets and an umbrella hanging up neatly on pegs by the front door. A little mid-century shoe rack. Handmade ceramic bowls and plates in her kitchen, glazed in organic shaped black-and-white polka dots. I couldn't even muster the energy to be jealous. It was all outside the realm of what I considered normal living accommodations.

"I can't wait to see what you think of this film," she said. "You always immediately notice the one thing the artist hopes you won't notice."

She gave me white wine in a handmade porcelain one-of-a-kind mug and I held it carefully in both hands as we watched the film. Maybe because of the surveillance focus of the film, I felt a bit paranoid. I tried to understand the reason I was invited by Suz to watch it.

She paused the film without saying anything, got up, and came back with a bag of Flamin' Hot Cheetos. And from that point on I loved her.

At home I looked up "Laura Owens art." I was tired of not recognizing any of the names people around me used with ease. I was tired of having to sit silently during discussions about art because I couldn't even use context cues to figure out what medium an artist worked in.

I found a web page cataloguing some of her pieces. I was expecting to be annoyed. I guess I was already annoyed and was seeking out more concrete reasons to justify the feeling. I scanned the images aggressively, trying to find labels, as if it were an Art History quiz and I only needed to memorize the right answer, not learn anything. But the work defied any label I thought to give it. Every time I came up with one, the next piece wouldn't fit in with it at all. Some were childlike, some were abstract, one political or sports-related and in reference to M. C. Escher, one looked like a fashion illustration done by a high schooler, some had 3-D elements. Some looked sloppy, but I could tell from others that she had a lot of technical skill, so the sloppiness must have been a choice. The paintings were all in different styles, as if being identifiable was not the goal, and the concept dictated the approach and not the other way around.

I was kind of mad that I liked it, that my taste aligned with Charlene's, that she had given me something by introducing me to this artist.

Do you know the artist laura owens, I texted Benji.

Yeah! She is awesome, he wrote back.

Just discovering rn, I texted.

Oh man, lucky, he wrote.

I threw my phone across the room.

Remake of *Rushmore* but the whole movie happens in one room and the lighting is bad and there are no lines.

Remake of *Rushmore* but it's just a video of my face as I try to mimic the actors in real time as I watch the movie for the first time.

Remake of *Rushmore* but it's low-quality clips and stills from the movie found on YouTube dubbed over by me improvising the dialogue.

Remake of *Rushmore* but it's just a video of me tearfully confessing what an awful idea this was for a film project.

Remake of *Rushmore* but I don't make it and don't think about it anymore and work on other things that are more interesting and fail my class and call it performance art.

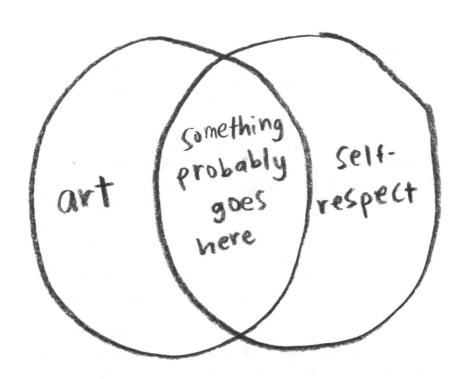

art | something probably goes here | self-respect

I hung three drawings of myself on the wall in Drawing II for critique. I had started making them at 1:00 that morning, stayed up half the night almost fully nude, in front of my full-length mirror, trying to push my limbs into interesting shapes.

Me, to a classmate I didn't usually talk to, for no reason, "It's weird to think of our bodies as part of how we communicate."

Them, whoever, "Cassidy" maybe, in a disinterested tone, "Yeah . . ."

If my main goal was to be understood, I wouldn't have been in a drawing class, that's for sure. I would have gone into Interior Design, used my minimalist sensibilities to make a name for myself in a small town, teamed up with a successful home flipper and pitched a show to HGTV about flipping industrial lofts, fallen in love on air over the course of two seasons, given birth in the finale of season 4, pitched a second show about DIY décor to supplement my rapidly expanding lifestyle, and spent the entire length of every episode oversharing about my life to my eager-to-please guests. But being understood by my peers was only a tertiary goal, after being someone's most important friend and growing into someone who didn't spit out any food that contained raisins like a literal baby.

"There is so much sadness here," someone in class said about my work. "The thick black lines are harsh and careless, as though the artist is upset with their subject."

Me in a perfect world, *Well, brava on the psychological interpretation, bitch, but as we all know, both the "artist" and "subject" are me.*

Me in reality, almost inaudibly, "Mmhm."

"The lines are very expressive. I can almost hear the charcoal scraping against the paper."

As quickly as it started, my critique was over, and we moved on to some other student's work, their process, the emotions conveyed and not conveyed, etc., etc., as if the act of hanging drawings on a wall invited assumptions about an artist's unidentified weaknesses.

"There are a lot of cool tones," I said. "Which remind me of sadness."

Fucking genius interpretation, my inner monologue said.

"The palette is very emotionally wrought," someone else said, in agreement with my spoken contribution, and in disagreement with my inner monologue.

I saw Suz walk out of a classroom and turn a corner. I jogged to catch up with her.

"Hey!" I said.

"Hey! Walk to the library with me."

Suz hadn't looked at me, I noticed. Was that normal? I suddenly felt certain I couldn't prove that anyone had ever looked at me at any point in my life. Maybe she and I weren't even friends, and whenever I thought she was talking to me she was talking to someone just behind me, and I had simply misunderstood the direction of her eyes every time.

"Can I call you later? I've got to photocopy a bunch of stuff, then I'm meeting up with Charlene. She's gonna connect me with her Detroit friends who live and work in this huge warehouse space. They've converted part of it to a gallery and now they have shows there."

"That's awesome. Yeah. Call me later."

"Okay, I will."

I left the library and wandered around the halls. The building was weirdly empty for it being so close to finals week. I decided to take advantage of the emptiness and sit in the lounge by the senior studios, which was usually crowded but now basically empty except for two tiny black-haired women sitting together at a table eating out of Tupperware and not speaking. I took out my sketchbook and drew a few quick studies of them. I had to complete twenty-six more sketchbook pages before the end of the semester. Light poured in from the huge windows behind me, making everything glowy and surreal. I tried to capture this in graphite and achieved marginal success.

My phone vibrated in my pocket and I took it out excitedly, expecting it to be Suz. It was my mom.

"Can I borrow some money to get a bond to bail Jenny out?" Mom said instead of "Hi."

"She's in jail? I thought she was in Reno."

"Well, Reno has jails. Can you bring the money tonight?"

Innocently, earnestly, naively, I said, "What money?"

"Some of your loan money? I just need eight hundred dollars. As long as she's there I'm stuck figuring out how to take care of Brian and I've missed a lot of work. I'm going to lose my job. You'll get your money back."

"That's almost the rest of my money, Mom. I can't. How am I supposed to pay my rent next month? Can you ask Uncle Peter?"

"Peter? Come on. You're joking."

If Mom lost her job, it would not be because I didn't give her eight hundred dollars, it would be because Jenny left town suddenly, abandoning her child. But from my mom's perspective, not giving her the money would feel like an equally harsh blow, and would prove to her that her two children were both so selfish and entitled that they'd conspire to ruin her life in favor of their own whims and comforts.

"I don't understand why any of this is my problem. Jenny is always a bitch to me, and doesn't give a shit about any of my problems, and now I have to bail her out? Nobody would ask Jenny to help if it were me in this situation. I guess that's the benefit of completely fucking up your life. No one asks you for anything."

Intro graphics of MTV's hit new show Everyone Has Taken Care of Me My Entire Life Because I'm a Selfish Asshole Who Doesn't Give Them a Choice! *Starring Jenny!*

Jenny waves from a large pile of her own feces on stage left, smiling innocently.

The host, a man in a tuxedo with a big white smile, points to me and says, "All of this is somehow your responsibility!"

I stand silently in front of an audience of everyone I've ever known. I look up and see a banner that says RESPONSIBLE PARTY *floating down in front of me like the one that floats down in front of the T. rex at the end of* Jurassic Park.

"I don't know what else to do, Joey," Mom said softly.

Sometimes it felt like my empathy bank was depleted but if I tried I could usually muster up a little more.

"Fuck. Okay. I'll send a check out tomorrow."

"Joey, I can't wait for you to send a check, wait for it to come in the mail, wait for the bank to deposit it. Can you just come to Lodi and withdraw cash?"

"That would literally take like fifteen hours and cost thirty dollars. I'm busy."

"Oh, okay. You're busy. God knows no one else is busy. Just you. No one else has anything else going on, no worries or stresses or toddlers they're suddenly taking care of that shouldn't be their responsibility."

"I'll put it in the mail tonight. That's all I can do."

"This is a fucking nightmare," Mom said, and hung up.

AMAZING!
how I am able to find
the energy to be
self-deprecating when
my family thinks
I'm a rich snob.

"Hey, Joey!" Allen said, appearing out of nowhere as usual. His face shone like a plastic doll. "Beautiful day. Can you believe this light?" He twirled around like a princess, gesturing to the air around him. His vest caught wind and blew up like a cape. I imagined strangling him to death.

"No," I said, trying to hurry past. People like Allen were the problem. People who pretended to care, smiled like there was some reason to smile, and spouted generic platitudes like *What's the point of being negative* and *Everyone has family baggage, you're not alone, if you need someone to talk to, I'm here.*

"Everything okay?" He grabbed my shoulder in an attempt to slow me down.

"Don't touch me. I'm sick of you fucking smiling at me like we're friends or something. Who are you even? What is your job? I don't have the energy to feel bad about my interactions with you. I'm busy feeling bad about literally everything else in my life. Yes, the light is beautiful, what a day! Bleep bloop bleep!" I made a gesture like I was playing finger cymbals, an attempt to look like a robot that didn't make sense. But I kept speaking, words pouring out of my swollen throat like this was their only chance for escape.

"For a while I thought my sister might be dead but now I know that she's not, she's just in jail for reasons I'll have to look up on the internet to find out and she needs eight hundred dollars to get out, which my mom is pressuring me to give to her so that my sister can come home and take care of her child who she abandoned. So now on top of everything else I'm going to lose my apartment because I'm never going to be able to get a job in time to pay rent."

"I'm sorry, Joey. You know, the school offers free therapy sessions to students. I could see . . ."

I looked him straight in the eyes, did jazz hands (?), and said, "Fuck you, Allen."

how do you know what you like|　　　　　　　　　　🔍

marxism what is it	history
jennifer berry reno arrest	history
jobs that hire literally anybody	history
what is wrong with me quiz	history
linda nochlin books	history
feminism art theory	history
how to be more interested in your interests	history
how to prioritize your pointless art while sister is in jail due to public intoxication and mom might lose the only job anyone in family has because she was left to care for sister's abandoned child	history
cheap dinner that isn't beans	history

close

In the dark of my apartment, having failed to go to sleep for the last four hours, I considered how Allen might have felt after I yelled at him.

Uh, bad? my inner monologue offered, shrugging.

Maybe I couldn't empathize with other people's emotions because I was training myself to push my own emotions out of the way. Put them aside for another time. Or never. Did that have to be such a bad thing?

Maybe I could pour my emotions into my art instead of facing them directly.

Maybe my *Rushmore* remake was a metaphor for all the emotional work I refused to deal with. A documentation of the processes of my brain as it ignored every real issue it was dealt in favor of thinking about an art project that had no clear purpose.

This would have to be explained in some kind of supplementary text to the film. With a list of all the things I had neglected while making the film.

1. (I was going to list the things I was currently neglecting in life but why bother?)

Maybe this rampant neglect was not a sign of my weak personality after all but rather an artistic gesture representing art making as a way to remove oneself from one's own life. A self-referential statement about the process of making art and how pointless it is, but also, because of how pointless, how great. An *artistic interpretation* of a weak personality by an artist with an actually impressive command of her craft.

Maybe Art was Real Life and Real Life was Art.

Maybe I was having a breakthrough.

My *Rushmore* remake had the potential to be *too* good, too popular, expose me to the upper tiers of the art world before I was ready, solidify my reputation as an artist of a certain kind. Was this project what I wanted to be known for? Did I want this work to follow me around like a ghost for the rest of my life, being described in magazines and on the walls of art museum retrospectives I didn't even know were happening?

Idk.

I really d fucking k.

Maybe, I thought, I should release this project under a pseudonym so that later, when I did my real art, art I'd someday make that I actually understood, it would not be overshadowed by my *Rushmore* remake, which would inevitably, I was completely sure, be a breakout success. It was exciting but terrifying.

Drunk on beer and rosé from a gallery opening, I typed "the cast of Rushmore" into Google. This was not cheating; I was just trying to corroborate what I already knew about the movie. If that was even a word.

Corroborate. I need to corroborate the evidence. That sounded right.

I opened a bottle of Cook's champagne I had in the fridge and smelled the rim of the bottle. Art ideas can come from anywhere, even bottle rims. *You don't always have to be so self-critical. Just let the ideas flow.* This is something I would say to students when I went to their colleges to lecture about my creative process.

I clicked on Jenny's first mug shot on my web browser. It was the first image result after I typed "Jennifer Berry Lodi mug shot." In the photo, she looked scared, embarrassed, her cheek bruised. My first feeling was of embarrassment that I was related to her. Then I felt ashamed of myself for having that thought. Then I felt sad, first for her for having this shameful image out there in public, then sad for myself for not knowing how to help her, and not actually wanting to know how to help her. Then I felt ashamed that this image was something I had sought out, that I wanted to see her like this, that part of me wanted to feel these conflicting feelings.

I opened a new tab for Facebook and scrolled through Jenny's photos (other peoples' tattoos, acrylic French manicures, images of stupid quotes, a used makeup bag she was trying to sell for forty dollars) and status updates:

"All I want is someone to stay even tho how hard it is to be wit me."

"my baby got.me a family size bag of fritos that is true LOVE yall"

"parden me while I burst into flames"

"I feel sorry for you you had all my.love an blew it too kick it with a lil girl with NO ass bahaha"

I was surprised at how many of her vague posts seemed romantic. Were they about Lucas? Someone else? I was ashamed to realize I had never considered that she was in love with Lucas, even though she had been on and off with him for years and they had a baby together. Did I think she was incapable of feelings, or was it simply that I had never thought about it at all? I tried to imagine what she looked like when she posted these things; coming home, getting on the computer in Mom's dining room, typing her post. In my head, she looked angry.

I went to my own profile, trying to see it from Jenny's perspective: in-progress drawings, bathroom selfies, art books open to my favorite pages, strange compositions of nature, and status updates so vague I couldn't even decipher them myself, like, "I have never been in the mood for talking." (*?? Okay?*) Jenny would not wonder what I meant. She would not take a moment out of her life to worry about me.

Or maybe I was just oblivious to the ways she cared about me, like I was oblivious to so many other things.

Allen was talking to a student near the entry to where my film class was held. I sat on a bench and pretended something was happening on my phone and waited for him to walk away so I wouldn't have to pass him on my way into class.

I texted Suz: *you in class already?*

I tried to remember what I had said to him but I couldn't remember a single word. I could only remember my anger, how ugly I sounded, how close I was to crying.

Micah walked up to me and sat down next to me.

He said, "Do you want to go to a show with me at the Rickshaw Stop?"

"Tonight?"

"Yeah. Like eleven."

He and his girlfriend had broken up again, I guessed. There was a certain charm in being the backup girl. Very little to lose. Very little to gain. Very little to wonder about.

"Um, maybe," I said. "Can I let you know later? Probably. I have to double-check something."

"Yeah, yeah. No pressure. It should be fun though."

"Okay, I'll just text you later."

I looked up and made brief, excruciating eye contact with Allen, and quickly looked back at Micah.

"All right, cool," he said. "Talk to you later. Or see you later."

"Yeah, probably."

After he walked away, I looked back at my phone and there was a text from Suz: *I'm not coming to class today. working in the library. tell me what I miss?*

I texted Suz: *Oh, okay. Do you want to hang out tonight? Sleepover?*

I sat there waiting for either Suz to text back or Allen to leave my sight, and eventually Allen walked away and I bowed into the darkened film class ten minutes late to watch Larissa's final project, in which she recorded herself reading one sentence of a prewritten statement about being abused over the course of three weeks.

I saw Suz and Freddie approaching the library exit as I walked in.

Suz said, "I am a *woman* making *art* but I reject the label *Woman Artist*. The implication is that artists are men by default."

Freddie said, "But without the label how are we supposed to know whose work is worth less money?"

She elbowed him playfully.

"Hey!" I said.

"Oh, hey, Joey," Suz said.

I tried to gauge whether she seemed happy to see me. "Do you guys want to hang out tonight? Micah invited me to a show that sounds cool."

"An opening?" Freddie said.

"I think a music show," I said.

Freddie turned to look at Suz in a long, strange way, his eyes rapidly moving across her face.

"Oh, we can't," Suz said. "I'm . . . We're . . ." She and Freddie continued looking at each other, smirking. "Um," she said, still trying to finish the sentence.

"Okay, that's enough. Gross. Have fun."

I went to the textbook section to find the modern art book that was a required purchase for Art History but that I did not buy, opting, instead to do the required reading in the library every week (it was not possible to check the book out), but it wasn't on the shelf, it was in someone's lap as they sat on one of the couches reading a different book about Francis Bacon.

The implication in being called a Woman Artist, I thought, is that someone thinks you're an artist.

Watching Micah's face change in bursts in the strobe light at a punk show, I felt something electric. He looked like panels in a comic, or a series of shots taken by paparazzi, both of which assume a level of interest in the slight mundane changes a person's body makes by being in the world. The assumption itself is part of what is interesting. You need to know why someone thinks this is interesting, or why they find it interesting, and so you are interested. But Micah sucked. I could see that clearly even in the strobe. He acted entitled. He never asked me anything about myself. He badly needed to wash his hair. But it was easy to hang out with someone I didn't care about.

Micah caught me staring and I smiled. He probably thought I was in love with him, which was fine. It would work in my favor. He would think he could get anything he wanted from me. That perceived power over me would make me irresistible to him. Which would give me the power. I would not use it. I would simply enjoy having it.

"Do you want another drink?" he said.

"Sure," I said.

We walked away from the stage to the back of the room where there was a man selling cans of PBR out of a box on the floor. Micah handed him a five-dollar bill and the man gave him two warm cans.

"Isn't this band awesome?" Micah said, handing me one.

I considered how I wanted to answer. I had been waiting eagerly for each song to end, wishing a little wish each time the vocals dropped that the instruments would stop soon after. My heart dropped each time the vocalist started screaming again.

I don't really like music, I thought of saying. Or, *Are we supposed to stand here the whole time?*

"They're tight," I ended up deciding to say.

"I know, right?"

We took the BART back to Mission and then walked to Micah's apartment. We lived pretty close to each other, it turned out.

"Welcome to my humble abode," he said.

There was a gun on the floor by a video game console, which was resting on top of what appeared to be a pair of men's boxers. Above the TV was a poster-sized illustration of Biggie hanging with a single tack, curled significantly at the corners. There was a thick smell of weed and coffee and garbage.

"This is Trevor," Micah said, pointing to a skinny person being consumed by both his hoodie and the couch cushions.

"Hey," I said. Trevor nodded.

I motioned to what I saw was the bathroom and locked myself in, breathing shallowly. I sat on the toilet and looked out the window remembering, out of nowhere, a fear I had as a child about talking in my sleep. I feared I would unknowingly reveal all my secrets to my friends at sleepovers, that my friends wouldn't tell me what I had said, and I would have no way of knowing what or how much they knew. I felt panic thinking of the possibility that I wouldn't be able to defend myself or claim that what I had said in my sleep was purely a dream-based fabrication and did not reveal embarrassing truths about my core self.

When I left the bathroom, Micah was playing a video game with Trevor.

I sat near the gun and watched the TV. A split screen showed two men running around killing people. I braided my hair as I watched.

When I was nine, I went to a sleepover at Lindsay's house. Her new friend Madeline was also there. When it was time for bed, I decided to stay awake until they were asleep, so that if I talked in my sleep, they wouldn't be awake to hear it. Once they were asleep, it occurred to me that one of them might sleep talk, so I stayed awake listening, waiting for them to reveal to me their most closely guarded secrets.

I became what I most feared, I thought, next to a gun, eleven years later.

To-do list for today

- Write a three-page analysis about how cognitive dissonance relates to modern art

- Find something to eat that is free or under a dollar

- Job (get one)

I texted Suz to see if she wanted to meet up and work in our sketch-books together. I was behind by several days and had to turn it in for final review the next Monday. Not that I was worried about pass-ing Drawing II. "You're all getting A's," Professor Long had said the first day of class. "If you don't take individual responsibility to do your assignments and progress your work, ask yourself why you're at fucking art school."

But Suz texted back saying she was at a gas station in Los Banos. She was driving to Los Angeles with Herta to go to Herta's stepbrother's art opening. It was some kind of large installation piece showing at some gallery that Suz seemed impressed by. I had never heard of it, but I had never heard of a lot of things.

Charlene is going to be in LA, too, Suz texted, guiltily I thought. *For work-related reasons.* But they would see each other at the show, be-cause she actually already knew Herta's stepbrother.

Good, I texted.

Good, I thought. *Suz is going to LA and she's going to Detroit and she never tells me anything because we are such good friends and good friends don't need to talk to each other to prove they are friends. Friends can just relax and not know anything about one another and make up whatever truths they want for as long as it feels convenient and then when the time is right they can fuck off forever.*

I would have invited you but I know ya have a lot going on :-), she texted.

Very true, I texted.

I looked through Suz's Facebook page: a long scroll of art (mostly by others); short poetic text posts ("a garden of internets that all need to be nurtured differently"); nature stuff from confusing perspectives; a link to a book called *Natural Bust Enlargement with Total Mind Power*; a link to a song by R. Stevie Moore; a link to a song by Billie Holiday; a photo of a twelve-pack of Red Bull on a table in her painting studio; birthday messages she didn't like or respond to; and a sprinkling of gorgeous photos of her posted by other people: one of her sitting cross-legged on the floor with a video game controller wearing glasses I'd never seen her wear; another in front of a body of water, smiling sweetly but looking down instead of at the camera, her curly bangs blowing away from her forehead, her red thermal shirt cajoling me to buy one just like it. The comments were always the same: "you are gorgeous!" "please come visit me," "this photo makes me so happy," "dying from your beauty," but never a reply from Suz. I scrolled to find another photo, this one where she was slumped over suitcases in an airport, recognizable to me by the style of carpet, not that I'd ever been in an airport myself. In this one she seemed famous already, aware that she was being watched by strangers yet confident enough to slump weirdly over suitcases, her limbs pointing in odd directions as if she were playing a suitcase version of Twister. She had posted this photo herself eight months before and captioned it, "always try to be the best version of yrself." This was from around the time I had met her.

I scrolled back up and clicked on the link to the R. Stevie Moore video. She had posted it six weeks ago, at the start of the semester. It was called "There Is No God in America." I watched it three times, looking for clues to Suz's intention in sharing it. It had the quality of something that intended itself to be obscure. There was video of clouds superimposed over the animation that I initially mistook for glare on my screen.

I imagined Suz driving into LA with Herta and Charlene, laughing, windows down, recalling facts about art history, agreeing with each other about what is cool and what is pathetic and what is intellectually interesting but formally bad, showing up at art venues with a breadth of knowledge and understanding about who has shown there before, who has been seen buying art there. I was glad I wasn't with them.

On Sunday morning I walked to school to print out an essay for Art History about impressionism that I had titled "Impressions of Impressionism," which had been funny to me at 3:45 a.m. but stupid and embarrassing at 9:00 a.m. As I arrived, I got a text from Mom that contained a selfie of her and some guy I didn't recognize, both shiny and smiling drunkenly, followed by a text: *Steve took me out for dinner tonight. I felt pretty.*

I pressed the crosswalk button and texted: *Did Jenny come back?*

Mom texted: *Not yet. shes out of jail and said shes coming home. I looked up bus schedules and sent them to her. I told her if shes not back by this weekend I'm dropping brian off at his fathers.*

I texted: *His fathers . . . what? his box behind safeway?*

She texted: *Well his moms where hes been staying I guess*

I texted: *where is brian now*

Mom texted: *Steves daughter lauren is babysitting for a few hours and then leanne is.picking him up and dropping him off at my work*

I texted: *Ok well don't take him to lucas moms house. Jesus. We'll never see him again*

I put my phone on silent and tossed it in my bag.

The last time I saw Lucas was outside Safeway a year and a half ago, before I left for college. I had taken Jenny to see him there because he was living in the bushes behind the parking lot.

The time I saw him before that, he was not yet living behind the Safeway parking lot. I drove Jenny and Brian to a doctor's appointment, and we went to Lucas's apartment afterward and he promptly left, saying he would be right back, and never returned.

The time I saw him before that was at the hospital after Brian was born. He arrived three hours after the baby came, and immediately started arguing with Jenny about money. He owed somebody who bought him food the night before, and they were waiting in the hospital lobby for money.

The time I saw him before that, he was at our house waiting for Jenny to come home. He started yelling racist things out our living room window in the direction of our Black neighbors. He wouldn't shut up or leave when I asked him to. I called Mom at work because I didn't know what to do, but she couldn't come to the phone, so then I called the cops.

A few hours later, I looked at my phone and saw that I had a text that read, *Going to reno to pick Jenny up at a truck stop. If Jenny calls you tell her to stay where we agreed to meet at ok. Im tired as hell only got 4 hours sleep Brian was up all night*

I texted: *Ok damn, that's a long trip. But glad she's coming home!*

Mom texted: *Yea its long im tired its been one tantrum after aother can you call jenny and remind her to be at the truck stop right at 3 I don't want to wait around leaving now*

I texted *Ok* but knew I wouldn't text Jenny. If anything, a reminder from me would likely ensure that she wouldn't be where she said she would be.

SF bay area > san francisco > jobs > art/media/design

Seeking illustrator (remote)

experience artist wanted to paint detailed image i have in my
head of my wife when she was 22 (she passed 8 months ago) as i
will describe. I do0nt have any photos of her at this time so this
would be a special project for me to remember her. She was a very
beautiful wonderful woman and I miss her. Her face is clear in my
mind, i just want to see her again Please sent a portfolio of other
work like this you have done so I can get an idea of how you can
bring this memory to life

- Principals only. Recruiters, please don't contact this job poster.
- do NOT contact us with unsolicited services or offers

The act of not working on *Rushmore* was an artistic gesture. Everyone I came into contact with was experiencing my art practice.

The thoughts inside my head thought they would escape someday, but they would not.

I would trap them forever inside my skull, deprive them of new sources of information, let them cannibalistically feed on each other, growing more and more uncertain of their purpose, never letting them be seen or heard or judged by another living soul, all of my individual thoughts living together in their skull interior commune to fester, manipulate each other, discover themselves, talk endlessly about what they wanted to do but never actually would.

I should get an MRI scan of my brain, I thought, hang it on the wall, and be like, *look, they're separating themselves into a hierarchy,* and everyone would be like, . . . *who?* And I'd be like, *my thoughts about* Rushmore. *They're forming a government. They're developing a system of voting that doesn't treat each vote as equal. They're giving power to those who most want it.* I'd leave out the part about them cannibalistically feeding on each other. *They're doing absolutely everything they can to avoid starting this* Rushmore *remake.*

"A lot of 'great art' sucks." —Me trying to make myself feel better about my art sucking.

"Maybe art *should* suck." —Me trying to convince myself my art doesn't suck.

"At least I *know* my art sucks." —Me trying to gain a feeling of superiority over other artists, despite my art sucking (and knowing it).

"What does it mean to suck?" —Me trying to appear intellectual to an audience that already knows I suck.

"Making art that sucks is the only path to making art that doesn't suck." —Me not making art.

I ordered a Thai bubble tea and sat at the window table with it. I texted my mom: *Did you make it to Reno?*

In some ways, I hoped my mom would not be able to find Jenny, that she was gone forever. Vanished in some magical, nonviolent way. It would make things very hard at first, but then, I think, it would make things easier.

Guilt over the emotional outcomes of hypothetical situations is not productive, I thought, feeling a creeping guilt imagining the happiness of my sister's disappearance.

Yep shes not where were suppose to meet at, car is making a weird sound i think the engine is having.problem have to find a.mechanic when I get home, just what i dont need alwayws something, Mom texted back, followed by, *at a walmart buying Pepsi its really hot here today*

I wondered if Jenny knew what bubble tea was or if she ever worried about anyone the way I worried about her.

My mom picked Jenny up from Reno uneventfully. "Uneventfully" in this case meaning that my mom worked a half day and drove to Reno afterward, then Jenny wasn't at the spot she was supposed to be, leaving my mom and Brian waiting there for two hours, until she finally picked up the phone (didn't call back—finally picked up) and gave my mom the address of a different location across town, actually waited at this second location, and got into my mom's car without screaming at her. I had placed my phone upright on my easel so I could see the real-time text updates throughout Drawing II. We were using experimental tools to apply ink to paper. I had brought in several thin sticks I had found in my neighborhood that morning. They gave me unreliable, scratchy lines that I didn't like. We then thought of descriptive words to use to describe the marks we made.

"Angsty," someone said.

"Milky. Gooey," someone said.

"Gothic. Regal."

Brians hungry and jenny says she hasnt eaten in 3 days. were going to stop abd get burgers then goin home, my mom texted.

It's funny that the world just keeps going. Seems impossible that there hasn't been a moment yet where humanity is collectively like, *Can we pause for a sec and reassess what we are doing here? Cuz something feels off.*

"Coarse," I said when it was my turn. "Antagonizing."

There was a woman outside of Safeway with a sign that read *any-thing helps*. She looked only a little older than me, unbathed and inattentive of the action of the parking lot, in a pink crop top, jeans, and red Converse.

I remembered seeing Jenny asking for money outside of Kmart when I knew she had somewhere to go, knew our house had food and toothpaste and designated Jenny drawers stuffed with her ugly clothes. There must have been other things she wanted. Drugs, I always thought, and still believed. I could be pretty unimaginative.

But it was conceivable that this woman was different from my sister, that she had other reasons for wanting money. There was a bill to pay, a phone plan expiring, a young boy at home who had never experienced Play-Doh. Maybe she was hungry, lacking the nutrients necessary for a life spent outdoors, or any number of other possibilities that weren't any of my business.

I'd be happy to get something for you, I imagined saying to this woman. "Is there anything in particular you need?"

I said nothing and walked past her into the store, fantasizing about things I might purchase for her. A comically large turkey sandwich from the deli, a bottle of water, tampons, a baguette, pretzel M&M'S, no, peanut M&M'S, no, both.

For my lunch I picked out a yogurt from the discount dairy bin and a box of granola. I paid for them with a ten-dollar bill and got $6.57 in change. I thought about giving the woman the five-dollar bill, but it was a lot to part with, more than I had spent on my own meal, then I thought about giving her the one-dollar bill, then I wondered if giving her fifty-seven cents would be insulting or even a burden, and that was how easy it was to make not helping at all the most rational decision, and then I was many yards past her walking toward campus thinking about a movie I had never seen.

Benji and I went to a night lecture on campus by a comic artist he liked. He drove us back to his apartment and we watched an animated movie that the comic artist had cited as inspiration and then had quick, uncomplicated sex. Spooning on his filthy bed in afterglow, he ran his fingers through my hair and I thought, *maybe his landlord would allow me to move in with him.*

"I'm not a puppy," I said, mimicking something I once witnessed a hot girl say flirtatiously to her boyfriend after he called her "cute." It didn't have the same effect in this context, and seemed to piss Benji off. He took his hands out of my hair and got up and turned on some unpleasant, percussive music and started emptying his pencil case onto the ground, organizing the pencils into rows, his thick brow aimed down, obscuring his eyes.

"What is this music?" I said.

"If you don't like it, change it."

"No, it's interesting."

"Okay."

I listened carefully, trying to think of something else to say.

"It almost sounds spooky," I said.

"Okay," he said.

"Do you want me to leave?" I said.

"Not at all," he said unconvincingly.

"I should go anyway," I said. It was 2:00 a.m. and I didn't want to go. I lingered a bit, gathering my things and pretending to look around for something in his sheets, hoping for an offer to drive me home or an invitation to stay after all.

"All right," I said.

"All right," he said. And I left.

Something Benji Said

The thing about having a penis is you can measure it at any time

but once you do

then you'll always know

Idea for a Series of Drawings

[Me opening my apartment door at 3:00 a.m. to reveal everything exactly as I left it at 9:00 a.m.]

[The light is coming from the streetlight in the alley behind me, which illuminates the back of my head and every individual strand of my tangled, unwashed hair.]

[Full-body portrait of me bringing my bike into the apartment and leaning it against the wall by the door. The overhead lights have been turned on but they're not very bright. Muted gray color palette.]

[Close-up portrait of me taking my shoes off, which somehow suggests a feeling of sadness that the viewer isn't sure how to place. Is it because the shoes are in terrible shape? Because some subtle facial gesture reveals that the subject (me) is struggling emotionally? Because shoe removal is usually performed without witness, so the act of observing it feels invasive and unwelcome and somehow emblematic of the viewer's own loneliness and pain?]

[Me eating Cup O' Noodles, bathed in laptop light.]

I found a letter taped to the front of my door when I left my apartment in the morning, which was not where I usually received mail. The letter also wasn't addressed. It read:

Joelle Berry,

I am writing to inform you that we did not receive payment for your April rent, which was due by April 5.

Per the terms in our lease agreement, I have added a $75 late fee to your account. Your total amount due is now $850. Please drop off your check to the office by the end of the day tomorrow.

Sincerely,

Ken Schlemp

I called Mom on my way to class the next morning.

"How is it having Jenny home? Everything back to normal?"

"Yeah, it's a big relief," Mom said. She sighed heavily, helping illustrate to her emotionally barren daughter that her level of relief was high.

I felt compassion for my mom rise up into the middle part of my chest and then stop, reaching its limit.

"Lucas is staying with us now, too," she said.

I almost laughed. Instead I stopped breathing, said nothing, and looked into the lens of the camera that was resting on my desk as if it were documenting my reaction.

"I know," Mom said. "But he's supposedly got a job starting next week. And when Jenny gets a job she'll need someone to watch Brian. I can't be responsible for him all the time. Her being gone almost broke me. They need to figure out how they can raise this baby together."

"You remember what happened last time, right? How he kept bringing crackheads over in the middle of the night? How he fell asleep on the kitchen floor with breakfast sausage cooking on the stove burner without a pan?" I said these things to my mom in a way that implied she had done them, that they were not Lucas's fault or Jenny's responsibility or even terrible things that simply had happened to us. I said them as if they were her personal failings, things she had decided to do to herself again.

"I know," she said, resigned. "I told them I wasn't going to put up with it this time."

"Okay, well that should do it," I said.

"It's such a beautiful day," Mom said, changing the subject. "I just want to be outside."

And then, "I'm going to send you a big thing of protein powder. I bought it but I don't like the taste of it."

Drawing II class was about how to talk about drawings, not about how to draw. For some reason, I was expecting to learn new drawing techniques in a class called Drawing II. A silly presumption. We were expected to make work outside of class time, in our own studio spaces, to bring works in progress to hang on the walls and discuss when our class met every Monday, even though we usually only got around to looking at three or four students' work. I had brought with me a self-portrait done in purple tones. It was unimaginative work, and I hoped that I would not have to present this week, so I would have time to start a new drawing before it was my turn for crit. It seemed increasingly likely that I would not have to show, since everyone was engaged in a discussion about a pen and ink piece of Herta's and class time was running out.

"What do the lemons over the knees represent?" Andrew said.

"Oranges," Herta said sarcastically. After a moment she said, "They're lemons. They don't represent something else."

"What do the lemons *mean*?" Andrew said. "Why are they there?"

You could tell Andrew wanted everyone to know that he thought about symbolism quite a lot. His own work was always symbol-heavy, in obvious, boring ways. Once he presented a drawing of a teddy bear with big glossy eyes that reflected flames. "The flames symbolize the death of childhood," he had said. I would have liked it as a drawing, I thought, if I didn't know about the symbolism.

After a long silence, Herta said, "Sometimes kneecaps look like lemons to me."

"Then do they represent your relationship to anatomy?" Andrew offered helpfully.

"I view them as symbols for how vulnerable our bodies are," another student named Marc said.

Herta shrugged, frowned, and shook her head. She looked kind of pissed off about how the conversation was going. I wished I were like her. I wished I could be angry when people didn't immediately recognize the greatness of my work, instead of ashamed.

"It is okay to not always know what your work symbolizes," Professor Long said. "But it is important to engage with your work as you make it, and to question your artistic impulses and figure out why you made the choices you made so that you can begin to find meaning in your work."

"I don't know if I'm looking for meaning," Herta said.

"It's our job as artists to dissect the meaning in our own work," Professor Long said.

Andrew nodded enthusiastically.

"I don't know if I agree with that. I would say that's the critic's job," Herta said.

"But if we aren't aware of the meanings in our work, we cannot talk about it," Professor Long said. I noticed defensiveness in his voice.

"Why do we need to talk about it?" Herta said. "Why does the artist have to be part of the conversation? I do not consider myself an art critic."

I was impressed by this notion. I, too, did not want to be involved in the conversation about my work. It was too much pressure, on top of having an idea and conjuring the confidence and patience to carry it out, to figure out its meaning or value to the world while it was still being made.

Didn't it make more sense to allow the viewer to determine the meaning for themselves? If artistic intent was more important than what the work made a viewer feel, why go through the trouble of making art at all? Why not write essays or release statements explaining how certain images can symbolize other things, and skip the art making?

"We are actually the most important critic our work has," Andrew said.

"Okay," Herta said.

"What if it takes us a long time to figure out why we're making what we're making?" I said, the third or fourth time I'd spoken in this class all semester. "We should be allowed to express ourselves without knowing exactly what we're expressing."

"It's not about being allowed to do one thing or another," Long said. "Of course you don't need permission to make art in a certain way. What I'm suggesting is that you analyze your artistic inclinations as . . ."

I stopped processing the content of Long's words as I felt myself turning red. Of course I hadn't meant "allowed" in the sense of some invisible rule maker holding an artist to a certain way of making art. I meant it more like, *Why should the artist ever be expected to lead the conversation about their own work?* or *Is art going to be interesting if the artist is making art as if it's a crossword puzzle with a set of predetermined answers?* I regretted including myself in the conversation and wondered why I had done it. I looked at Herta, whose expression was a strange combination of interest and boredom as she stared out the window.

I met Micah for a show at Bottom of the Hill. I brought my laptop and a few sketchbooks and a couple of shirts in my backpack in case my landlord changed the locks while I was out. I knew it was probably illegal for them to change the locks before formally evicting me, but I also knew that they probably knew I wouldn't have the money to hire a lawyer.

The band started all at once, without even a drumstick countdown. It was loud and energetic, and, though I hadn't been making any noise whatsoever, I felt fully silenced by the spectacle. My brain had stopped whatever little background activities it was doing and focused on the performance. The musicians were washed in bright pink and red lights, which made their long unwashed hair and ratty clothes look synthetic, like candy. Their facial expressions ranged from bored to annoyed, but their music was chaotic, wild, beautiful. I don't think I even blinked during their entire first song.

"What is this band called, again?" I yelled to Micah.

"Acid Mothers Temple."

The music didn't stop between songs, but was continued by a single band member, in a solo bass line or weird, long, abstract vocalization, and then the rest of the band would join in again, simultaneously, without looking at each other, each person appearing perturbed by their own inner thoughts, grimacing, scowling, eyes rolling, at complete odds visually with the magic of the music they were creating.

I watched each musician individually, in awe but also in fear that I was missing something one of the others was doing. I understood, finally, deeply, for once in my damn life, the appeal of being a roadie.

I wanted to be able to soak in every moment. I wanted to know what facial expressions each band member was making without necessarily having to look at them. I wanted to know if they were grumpy or if that was just how their faces looked. I wanted to know how they felt about each other, if the closeness I was perceiving was closeness they felt or if it was an illusion caused by the magic of performance.

The music ended after what, to me, could have been any amount of time. Hours. Days. Months.

I bought a CD, wanting something to take home with me.

"That was sick," Micah said. The implausibility of walking home with Micah, a person who failed to interest me in any way yet who I still hung out with regularly, on a night like this, after being so deeply moved for what felt like the first time, was, somehow, poignant to me. It made me think about how nothing in life fit together. Nothing was supposed to be any certain way. Nothing was meant to work or make sense.

"I have never been more moved by a show," I said.

"Word," Micah said. "I'm glad you liked them. I didn't know this was your thing."

"Yeah, I didn't know either."

I finally checked my bank account and confirmed that I was almost out of money. I had $139.44. I was definitely not going to be able to pay my rent plus late fee. For some reason I hadn't processed that as "definite" yet. I hadn't tried hard enough to look for a job. I hadn't tried hard enough to live cheaply. I hadn't tried hard enough at anything.

I was going to have to put my furniture on the street and move back in with my mom, where I would sleep on the couch because Jenny and Brian were using our old room and there was no room for me because of all the boxes of old framed photos my mom somehow acquired.

Jenny would leave personal belongings on the couch and get mad at me when I moved them to sleep.

I would lie about my work experience and land my dream job: full-time Starbucks barista.

I would begin a summer romance with a coworker just so I wouldn't have to go home after my shift ended.

Mom would ask me for some unpredictable sum of money each month to help with bills and I would have to give it to her to avoid conflict.

I would spend many nights at my summer romance's apartment, where we would eat microwaved fish sticks and have long, deep, drunken discussions about *SpongeBob*. I would write these conversations down in my sketchbook, thinking there was a chance there was something artistically compelling about them but knowing, deep down inside, there was not.

I would get in trouble at work for wearing open-toed shoes and have my hours reduced to part-time.

Walking home by myself one night, I would look at the stars and think about how small and unimportant I was, how meaningless all my choices were against the backdrop of the universe. Clichés would feel profound, a realization so massive and complicated it would make me cry. No one would be home when I arrived, but there would be a pot of macaroni and cheese burning on the stove. I have always found the term *trailer trash* offensive because it's not the trailer's fault. The trailer does the best it can.

I would call Suz and try to describe my feelings about the stars and smallness and clichéness of it all, and would not be able to convey what I felt accurately, but Suz would say she understood what I meant, and the intellectual accommodation, the stooping to my level, would make me feel patronized and alienated and it wouldn't feel profound at all anymore, just sad.

My summer romance would fall in love with me and try to convince me not to go back to school, and instead move into his apartment near the KFC. I would fight with him about this if only because it was something to do, even though I didn't care what he wanted or thought.

Having saved almost no money over the summer, I would apply for more student loans so I could afford a deposit for another apartment near school. With roommates this time.

I would break up with my summer romance over the phone while eating Nachos BellGrande.

Mom's car battery would die and she'd ask me for the money to replace it so she wouldn't lose her job/livelihood/trailer/semblance of stability/belongings/pride/will to live.

My summer romance would tell all of our coworkers what I said about them behind their backs, leaving out the fact that we had shit-talked them together, and the whole group of them would create an informal campaign to sabotage me and get me fired. The manager, understanding that I was being unfairly sabotaged by my coworkers but not seeing any benefit in taking my side, would fire me for coming back from lunch two minutes late, citing my previous open-toed shoe issue as my first and only warning.

When I got home from my last day at Starbucks, Mom would be crying. At first she'd tell me to leave her alone, but then she'd immediately start explaining where she had expected her life to go and how wildly that had diverged from where she had arrived instead. She would tell a long anecdote about a time when she was a teenager and her dad had got drunk and told her that her aspirations to be a nurse would never be realized, that she might as well give up now because she would end up a sad old drunk like everyone else in their family. I would not interrupt her to tell her that I'd already heard that story several times, instead deciding to sit next to her and awkwardly touch her wrist. She would go on to say the discouragement only made her want to be a nurse even more, for all the reasons she had told me before, but also, now, to prove her dad wrong, to prove that he was a fool who couldn't see the value in her. She'd use a hand gesture she didn't often use and my fingers would drop away from her wrist. It would occur to me that she made the hand gesture only to get me to stop touching her. *But he was right*, she'd tell me, as if just realizing in the moment that she didn't end up a nurse after all, only a phlebotomist. *You could go back to school*, I'd say, and she'd leave the room without saying anything more.

Suz would call to tell me about an art show in Chicago she got a film piece accepted into, curated by somebody she'd expect me to recognize the name of. She'd be flying there for the opening, she'd tell me, right before the next semester started. She would ask what I'd been working on over the summer. I'd think about the notes I took about the *SpongeBob* conversations I had with my summer romance. *Some drawings*, I'd say. She'd be silent on the other end, waiting for actual information. *About aching*, I'd add, trying to seem poetic.

I would get a letter informing me that my student loan request had been denied unless I could produce a cosigner.

I'd apply for jobs in San Francisco and the larger Bay Area. If I could line up work, I'd think, maybe there was some way I could still move back to the city before school started, even if I couldn't enroll in classes.

I'd get called for an interview at a café in a remote part of San Francisco. I'd spend thirty dollars on a new outfit from Walmart and seventy-five dollars taking various buses to get from Lodi to the interview. The interview would go well. I would be charming and professional, and somehow, despite the many flaws in my personality that people normally recognized right away, the interviewer would like me. I'd spend a few nights at Suz's (a brief and chilling rediscovery of my rapidly disappearing former life) before heading back to Lodi. I would never hear back about the job.

The school semester would start back up without me. I'd begin looking for work in Lodi, planning to save money for the rest of the year
and re-enroll in the Spring.

Jenny would disappear again, and I would be tasked with looking after Brian. My job search would be put on hold. I'd decide to
be okay with that. I'd take Brian to the park every morning, and
to the library every afternoon. I'd cut his peanut butter and jelly
sandwiches into cute shapes with cookie cutters, and we'd take
naps in front of the TV, his little blond head nestled into my armpit, his baby scent warm and sweet. I would fantasize that I was his
mother and he was my baby and this was our little life together.
I'd start dinner before Mom got home each night, Brian happily
playing in the playpen I'd buy with my own money and set up in
the kitchen. I'd hand him little pieces of cucumber or cheese to
snack on while he waited for dinner. Mom would come home after
work, delighted by the peace of our home and at the quality of the
meal I'd made. She would still drink, but not as much. We would
have a beer together and talk about how Brian had started calling
me *Mama.*

"He's lucky to have you," she might say.

Jenny would come back in the midst of withdrawals. She'd lash out
at me for taking responsibility for Brian while she was gone, accus-
ing me of trying to brainwash him against her. She'd punch me, and
break my nose. I wouldn't go to the hospital, knowing my health
insurance had lapsed from being out of school. Mom would come
home and be angry with both of us for fighting. She'd threaten to
kick us both out, as if Jenny and I had played equal roles in the
drama. As if my nose had broken itself.

I'd call my summer romance at 11:30 p.m. after months of not seeing him and ask if I could come over. We'd rekindle our boring relationship.

Happily ever after.

I called Suz, which I didn't normally do. I felt desperate.

"Hey, I've been texting you all day. Want to go to McDonald's with me before class? I need chicken real quick."

"I'm stuffed. I just had lunch with Charlene," Suz said. "We're gonna grab a coffee. Want to come with?"

"No, thanks."

I bought a double cheeseburger (chicken was too expensive) and ate the entire thing while waiting for a crosswalk light to change.

It would be good if I moved home. Maybe struggling to keep up with people who were doing better than me in every way was making me miserable. Maybe I'd be happier if I wasn't trying to be happy. Maybe life would be easier if I just let it wash over me like a wave instead of trying to claw my way out through sand and muck in an attempt to get to a probably imaginary beach where one can supposedly view the waves of the ocean without being pummeled by them.

I decided I'd work on *Rushmore* the rest of the night. I could honestly probably get halfway done if I just sat down and worked on it for a few hours instead of endlessly thinking about working on it. First I'd make some tea, though, to get me in a good headspace. I decided I'd put a little whiskey in it to loosen myself up a bit, to be less inhibited about my ideas, but when I took the bottle out of the cupboard I noticed there was only about half a shot left. I walked to the corner store to quickly grab a new bottle of whiskey. The corner store was having a sale on some of the nicer brands of alcohol, which were boxed and came with branded glasses, which I wanted for some reason. These bottles of the nicer brands of alcohol were only a little more expensive than the cheap whiskey I had planned on getting, but were also slightly smaller bottles. But also came with the glasses. I stood in front of the display for a little while, making calculations, and in the end decided to get two bottles of the cheapest whiskey, a tier lower than the one I had originally planned on getting, because it turned out to be roughly the same price as one of the boxed alcohol sets, which I had somewhat rationalized buying, so I was actually being thrifty.

At home, finally at peace with my hot spiked tea, finally ready to be creative, I sat down and opened the document where I was taking notes for *Rushmore*.

I stared at the ficus tree outside my apartment window, nostalgic for the present moment. Soon I would be kicked out of my apartment, and I would never see this tree again. Certainly I would never see this side of the tree again as it was visible only from the inside of this apartment. I hadn't fully appreciated the tree, I now realized. I never gave it the consideration it deserved. I almost started crying thinking about how I didn't give the tree the attention it deserved while I still had the chance. Then I started feeling nostalgic about the *feeling* I was having about the tree. Would I ever be in a position again where I was about to lose so many things I cared about at once and able to project all those feelings onto a tree? I would miss this someday, when nothing was at stake and there was nothing in my life worth worrying about losing.

I turned my laptop around and took a picture of the tree using the built-in camera. The photo made the interior of my apartment look much darker than it did in life, my entire apartment a fuzzy gray frame around the tree, which showed up in greater detail than I had expected from a photo taken with a computer camera at 10:30 p.m. The streetlights shone from both sides, casting little geometric shadows on the leaves.

I walked to Walgreens, pretty drunk, to take a break and to pick up a few things that I had been meaning to get. I felt like I had already left San Francisco and was visiting it in a dream.

I didn't want to stop being the person I was becoming.

I didn't want to stop making art, even if I didn't understand why I was making it.

I didn't trust anyone who understood their own art.

What was art but a way to tell people to go away forever?

What was art but a one-sided argument that the artist started?

What was an artist but someone who wanted to be understood but didn't know how to communicate normally?

I agreed with my sister that I did not deserve what I had. What was I supposed to do with it, knowing I didn't deserve it, knowing I was lucky to get it, knowing I probably wouldn't get it again? Find ways to hate it? Let it slip away so I didn't have to feel guilty?

Could I sue whoever had first encouraged me to be artistic? I made a mental note to look it up on Law.com.

I made my way over to the checkout stands, and Allen was in line looking at the candy bar display. I inhaled comically loudly, and he turned to look at me. I was drunk enough that I momentarily believed if I stood there in silence and didn't breathe or blink, maybe he wouldn't see me.

"Hi, Joey," he said, looking away quickly.

His arm brushed by a Milky Way display as he turned away from me, and some of the bars dropped to the ground. I looked in his basket as he crouched to pick them up, which contained Gatorade, soy milk, blueberry muffins, a bag of socks, and a box of bandages. I felt a small amount of empathy surface, realizing that this whole time he had been a person who ate muffins and wore socks and not just an employee of the school.

"I'll take one of those," I said, enunciating dramatically and picking up one of the Milky Way bars he had stuffed back onto the shelf. Allen made a few quick fake-sounding laugh-adjacent noises and moved a little toward the register that still had customers in front of it. This was a way to physically distance himself from me.

"I think these are yummy," I said to the back of his head, and when he looked and smiled it occurred to me that he had been hired to be nice to me, and didn't love the job.

"Next," the cashier said.

Allen walked to the open register and didn't look at me again. Then, soon, it was my turn to check out and take my bag and walk back to my apartment alone.

Suz texted: *Please meet me for a drink? I know it's late. This month has been a whirlwind and I feel like we havent really hung out. I'm also freakingggg outttt about my life, the residency, blah blah blahhh*

She texted: *I'll buy!*

She texted: *I know a place that doesnt card*

I texted: *sure*

"I'm nervous about Detroit. I found out I'm the only woman who will be at the residency this summer, so, like, (a) I feel tokenized, and (b) I feel like I have to make hugely fucking exciting work while I'm there so the patriarchy knows how fucked it is. I want to make art so good that it makes them want to crawl into a hole and die. But that's a lot of pressure to put on myself."

"That fucking sucks," I said. "But doesn't it make you feel good that you're the one they want to tokenize?"

"No, it makes me feel fucking terrible. It makes me feel like there's only one spot for a woman and I took it, so I'm responsible for other women not getting that spot. It makes me feel like my work isn't actually valued for what it is and that my presence is only to benefit the optics of the program."

"Right," I said.

"And it's just such a bummer because I was really excited about it," she said. "And I began to realize that I'm excited to get out of San Francisco. I don't know. I'm claustrophobic here or something. So now I'm, like, I need to go to New York or LA, at least until I have a solid network. I don't know how artists make it in San Francisco. The galleries are just *blegh*. And the city is boring, too. I'm bored here. Aren't you bored?"

I shrugged, sipped from my whiskey ginger. To me, San Francisco was the entire universe; every other junky town just orbited around it.

"Charlene thinks there's a lot of potential here. And there's not any pressing need to move right this minute. New York is always gonna be there, right? I mean until the great flood or whatever." Suz noticed my whiskey ginger was gone and ordered another round, downing the rest of her Aviation in a single slurp. The degree to which the prospect of a new drink excited me was my warning that I was already drunk.

"Do you see yourself staying in San Francisco?"

"I have to move back home this summer," I said. My face flushed with heat in a comforting way, like hot water gushing into a cool bath. "I can't afford my apartment and I can't find a job. I'm worried that once I leave I'll never be able to get back."

"You should move into my room while I'm in Detroit," Suz said, digging through her purse and bringing out a small zippered bag that served as her wallet. "My parents paid for it through the end of the year. You can water my plants for me while I'm gone. God, Diana would love it."

She slid two dollars across the counter as a tip and smiled at the bartender.

I stared at her, in awe of the casualness in which she spoke these life-altering words.

"Wait, are you serious?" I said. "That would literally save my life, dude."

"Oh my god. Easy. Problem solved. You live in my room for the summer. I leave May 10, and the residency ends August 10, but I might go to New York for a week or two afterwards. You can stay the whole time. Part of the time. Whatever."

I'd wondered before what it felt like to win the lottery, the first few moments when you find out that your life has changed dramatically, that you're getting something most people can't fathom having. The feeling I was having must be close to that: a mental grabbing sensation, like you want to reach out to your winnings and tackle them to the ground before they skip away. An immediate sense of entitlement toward this thing that you've unexpectedly won. No joy. Just ownership. Followed, of course, by relief and shock and appreciation and all the things you'll later tell people you felt.

"All I ask is that you move my car once a week, to avoid street sweeping. You can use it, too."

I do not know how to drive, I thought about saying. But I didn't want her to change her mind.

"Did I tell you Charlene and Herta are dating now?" she said, changing the subject away from the profoundly important conversation I wanted to live in forever. "I feel like a matchmaker."

All night I kept waking myself up, remembering I could stay in Suz's apartment over the summer. I woke up exhausted, heavy, hungover. My body was trying to trick my brain into being depressed, into feeling guilty for my good fortune, but I couldn't. I felt too happy and thankful.

The key to success, I kept thinking, *is portraiture*. What would my life look like if I hadn't impressed my middle school classmates with drawings of our teachers, entered high school art competitions with pencil portraits of Jack Nicholson, gotten the attention of Lindsay's grandma who encouraged me to apply to art school, took the painting course where I met Suz?

What would I like about myself if I had never discovered my ability to sit with paper and pens for hours, determined to achieve a likeness? What would I think about?

I looked at the ficus outside my bedroom window, thinking again how it seemed to be a marker for this particular point in my life, how soon I would probably never see it again. But now that feeling was tinged in hope. I'd probably see other good things. I'd look back on this moment not as time I spent lacking in appreciation for the tree (let's keep believing this is about the tree) but appreciating the tree so much, feeling so undeserving of and ungrateful for the tree's presence in my life, that it made me fucking hate myself.

Those middle school drawings weren't the beginning, of course. In the beginning it was Jenny, *her* drawings, my admiration of her talent, the ease with which she worked, my desire to be like her. I have always been ashamed about my early awe of Jenny's art. I always felt like it was something I stole from her. It was hers and I liked it and then it was mine. The implication being that two artists can't exist simultaneously. That two sisters can't be interested in the same thing.

But I didn't take anything from Jenny. She introduced me to something that I liked. She made me see my life in a new way that made it better, which led me to other things that made it even better still, made *me* better, made me like the world more.

What would my life look like without Jenny?

BECOME AN EGG DONOR TODAY (berkeley)

Give the gift of life ! Egg donation is a beautiful way to help families who desire children, with many benefits to yourself as well.
Are you:

- A female age 21–35
- Non-smoker
- Non-drug user
- Attractive features
- Physically and psychologically healthy
- No family history of genetic disorders or mental illness
- Want extra money to travel or pay off debt?

Safe and private process. Being an egg donor provides you with genetic and fertility insight! We offer $6,000 per cycle. Apply now !

- Principals only. Recruiters, please don't contact this job poster.
- do NOT contact us with unsolicited services or offers

Eight days before my *Rushmore* thing was due, with nothing filmed, I took a bus to North Beach and walked along a street that consisted of fancy lady boutiques, considering the native civilizations that might have used this land for other purposes, once upon a time. The fact that our society was garbage was a comfort to me in times like these, when I was struggling with a problem whose outcome would ultimately have zero effect on anyone. Bad art < U.S. history. Bad art < mental illness. Bad art < human depravity. Etc.

I was hoping to be inspired. The camera I had borrowed from school was in my backpack in case the urge to create the thing I'd been avoiding creating for three months suddenly hit me in North Beach.

Every day I woke up and made the choice to keep doing this to myself.

LET'S JUST GET THIS OVER WITH, my brain would say. Making this art was my only shot at making it to the next part of life. The part where I didn't have to make the art I was making anymore.

I walked into a store that sold oversized scissors and resin-covered beetles, then I walked out of that store.

I walked into a café and, ignoring eye contact with the employees, went over to the bar and poured myself a glass of water. Then I went into the bathroom, which was clean and bright and had a small sitting area. I decided to take a break.

I opened my backpack, retrieved my Art History reader, and opened it to the section on abstract expressionism I was supposed to read before tomorrow. The first page showed a Rothko painting of a square, a black-and-white version of the same one that was printed on the cover of the reader in full color, showing it in its original reds and blacks. It evoked the alienation I felt at art school, the implicit expectation that I was supposed to be both cultured and educated, able to understand and appreciate art not by what it showed but by what I already knew about art and the world. Abstract art seemed designed for rich people. You were supposed to be impressed by the outrageous figure it sold for, moved by the nothingness you felt when looking at it, compare it favorably to all the other paintings in the world artlessly depicting things.

The caption under the painting read: *This and six other paintings were reclaimed by Rothko after seeing them on display in the Four Seasons restaurant. "Anybody who will eat that kind of food for those kind of prices will never look at a painting of mine," he reportedly said.*

I grunted unconsciously, surprised to be proven incorrect about something mere seconds after making an incorrect assumption about it.

I read on: *On finding inspiration for the Seagram murals from Michelangelo's staircase room he said, "He achieved just the kind of feeling that I'm after—he makes the viewers feel that they are trapped in a room where all the doors and windows are bricked up, so all they can do is butt their heads forever against the wall."*

This was a new concept to me: torturing rich people through art. Using work they viewed as property to own to make their lives worse. And to do it in such a way that they would still pay for the privilege.

A petite older woman who looked wealthy (pearl earrings, neatly styled hair, etc.) came in and I smiled at her, feeling a sort of love. For some reason the notion of antagonizing rich people made me feel more sympathetic to them: Rich people, they're morons like the rest of us!

But a few minutes later, a café employee came in and asked me if I was a customer.

"We've received complaints," she said.

I saw Diana talking on her phone outside a home goods store and waved to her casually. Unexpectedly, she ended her phone call and rushed across the street to hug me.

"Hey, new roomie!" she yelled.

She was on a break at work, she said. Did I want to get a taco with her? There was a great place at the end of the block that had several kinds of agua fresca. They also had great margaritas, if I was feeling up to it, although she had to go back to work so it probably wasn't such a great idea to drink too much. But if I wanted to, again, she would be down.

"Okay," I said. "Sure."

She wrapped her arm in mine and we walked down the sidewalk together like this. I didn't understand how physical closeness could come so easily to a person.

"I'm excited to live with you this summer," I said. "Thanks for agreeing to it. I missed rent on my apartment this month so I wasn't sure where I was going to go."

"Oh my god. No problem. I did not want to spend the summer by myself."

At the taco bar counter, I ordered chips and water and then heavily abused the salsa bar.

"Are you on a diet?" Diana said, watching me line up cups of salsa neatly on the table in front of me.

"No, I'm just really broke. I can't find a job. I feel like I need to find a food bank or something. Would that be fucked up of me to use a food bank?"

I looked into my cups of salsa, embarrassed. I shouldn't have said any of that. I had alienated the person I was going to live with, made her think I wanted to be pitied or given things, that I was someone who abused the system. Maybe she thought I wanted her to buy me food.

"Um," she said. "We're hiring at my work. It's not *cool*, but it's a job and it pays okay."

"What's the job?"

Diana nodded to communicate that she had heard my question. She had taken a large bite of burrito and I listened to a Maroon 5 song playing over the restaurant speakers as I waited for her to swallow.

Diana worked at Rose and Thorn, she told me, a lifestyle boutique up the street. She pointed through the wall of the taco shop. They were looking for another shop girl. She said the job would be easy and mostly consist of hanging out with her all day and assisting customers who knew they wanted to spend four hundred dollars but weren't sure on what. After lunch, she took me to the store to meet her boss, Cecily, who mentioned "artisanal linen" at least three times during our ten-minute chat, while I tried to sneak in tidbits about my nonexistent qualifications for working in a fancy lady store.

"I would personally never buy non-artisanal linen," I said. I wondered if I was selling myself too hard.

Cecily asked me to come in for training the following morning, then changed it to the following afternoon, when Diana would be working and could help train me.

All at once, on top of not having to leave San Francisco, I was employed. What did it feel like to win the lottery twice? Almost like I had expected it to happen. Almost like this was what the world owed me. My life was saved, it had required almost no effort, and no one else had seemed to notice the precipice I was being dragged away from. Was this what life was like for other people?

I went back to my apartment and immediately bought socks on-line. I'd been needing socks for months, my heels and toes poking through the few pairs of dingy gray ones I had (had the socks been white at some point or had I purchased gray socks? I legitimately couldn't remember), cold against the often-wet material of my shoes. Speaking of—I decided to order new shoes as well. I opened several tabs with shoes I wanted, comparing styles, prices, and versatility. I ended up buying two pairs. Two!

How was I supposed to continue to feel sorry for myself if I kept getting everything I wanted?

What if the secret to success was, instead of wallowing in self-pity, vocalizing the things I needed to people who had the ability to help?

What if, instead of feeling guilty about everything all the time, I just . . . didn't?

Although I recognize that's an easy perspective for the owner of multiple pairs of shoes to have.

Cecily and I spent two hours going over how to use the cash register, because she kept getting sidetracked by conversations with regular customers, which triggered long stories about her children's careers, various kinds of organic fibers, recipes she was hoping to someday steal from various local restaurants, and the broad idea of rain forest preservation (she was strongly for it). Then we went to the stock room and quickly looked at where extra merchandise was stored.

"There's basically no organization here, you just have to look and see what we have," she said.

She gave me fifty dollars cash for my "training" and scheduled me for thirty hours over the next two weeks, mostly on shifts with Diana.

"You can have as many hours as you want once the semester is over," she said.

The job was mostly to keep the store looking put-together while customers aimlessly walked through touching things, often while talking loudly on their phones. I'd walk through the store straightening kitchen towels and novelty tea strainers, or restock the odd room spray or enameled cast iron pot that had been sold. When our merchandise wasn't in slight disarray, and when customers weren't at our desk asking where exactly in Indonesia a baking dish had been made, I'd stand at the cash register looking at my phone or talking to Diana. Diana was actually pretty cool, I was discovering. I didn't know why I'd never noticed before.

"I can't believe I'm going to be twenty-one in a few days," she said. "I thought I'd have my shit together more by now."

Despite being nowhere near done with my *Rushmore* project and it being due in less than a week, I suggested doing something fun together for her birthday.

"That's such a good idea," Diana said, her eyes wide.

"We can have some people over to your roof. Mojitos?"

"Let's ride bikes through Golden Gate Park and then get ice cream on Haight and get pho and do karaoke."

"Even better," I said.

Over two years in middle school, I saved up sixty-five dollars by selling parts of my free hot lunch to other kids, looking for change on the ground wherever I went, and recycling soda cans and bottles from our garbage at the recycling center a few blocks from our house.

I decided to spend it and went on a shopping spree. I bought a fleece blanket with Shrek's face on it, a pair of sandals, and a box of Bioré pore strips.

Jenny was furious. She thought I was selfish for hoarding money while our family waited for food stamps that were never enough. While our mom, who had given us all we had, was forced to let her roots grow out, and while Jenny herself forwent buying a school yearbook. She took the issue up with our mom, who refused to take a side. Mom looked at me like she was trying to figure out why I was the way I was, how I could be so selfish when everyone else in the family was so good and pure. She didn't say I wasn't allowed to spend my own money, but she didn't defend my right to do so. If I could rationalize spending money without thinking of anyone else's needs, she said without saying, that was my burden to bear.

I remember trying to form an argument in my head to defend my purchases, unable to comprehend how conjuring something nice for myself out of literal garbage could be interpreted as selfish or mean, but also internalizing the fact that it indisputably was.

I can see now how a Shrek blanket could inspire frustration and anger. But I can also remember how nice it felt to give myself something that I wanted.

To be wrapped in the warm embrace of an ogre.

I've forgotten a lot of things, but not the feeling of that specific kind of comfort.

wassup, Micah texted.

wassup, I texted back.

Neither of us texted anything after that.

Jenny's name appeared on my phone while I was in the drawing studio, and I stepped outside to answer. It was highly unusual for Jenny to call me, and I considered the possible worst-case scenarios. Brian was in the hospital with a sudden illness. Mom had been murdered by "Steve," whom I had forgotten to look up on Facebook for personal details in case such a thing might happen. Lucas had kidnapped Brian and was asking for ransom.

"Hello?" I said.

"Hey," Jenny said. "Do you want to sell makeup? I just signed up to be a consultant and I need, well, this company is really, um, focused on women and success and stuff. The girl who I signed up through got a pink Cadillac from her business. It's great for someone like me, or like you, who isn't good at holding down a regular job."

"Oh, um. No, I don't really wear makeup. Where are you?"

From the main hallway, I could see it was raining outside, and I hadn't brought my rain jacket to school that day, only my sweater.

I crossed my bare arms, already cold thinking about riding my bike home in the rain.

"It's really easy to sell, Joey. This is a favor I'm doing for you. I've made a lot of freaking money already. I'm going to get my own place soon."

"That's great. So you're back at home now? How's that?"

"Yes," Jenny said, irritated, and I felt embarrassed to be transparently interested only in her whereabouts, as if all she was to me was a blinking dot on a map.

"Okay well do you want to just sign up and I'll sell it for you? If I don't get people to sign up, I'll get kicked out. It's only one hundred dollars to start. And then if your friends want to sell, then you get a portion of their sales, too."

"I already gave Mom money to bail you out. I'm broke."

"That was only like four hundred bucks."

"I gave her eight hundred."

"Okay, well I don't know what kind of *little deal* you did with Mom. But come on, it's gonna be really easy to make that money back plus commission if you get your friends to sign up, too."

"I'm not interested. I have to go, Jenny. Glad you're safe."

"My fucking god. You suck, Joey."

"Yeah," I said. "Well, talk to you later."

I hung up and waited, listening to my heartbeat, anticipating a wave of guilt and anxiety that didn't come.

I awoke to a series of comments from Jenny under a photo I'd posted on Facebook the night before of a drawing I had made of the ficus through my apartment window, a hint of my own face reflected in the glass among branches, that had gotten thirty-five likes.

I guess you like attention an feel like everyone owes you.something

You are so spoiled an act so superior

I got jack shit in life.

why are.you so bitter an angry?

your life doesnt matter

I clicked on the comment box and poised my fingers to type a response to her, but no response came. I didn't feel upset. I didn't feel insulted. My body was tired of reacting to stress. I considered deleting her comments. Or passive-aggressively liking them.

I took a screenshot of the post and comments. Maybe this was art. Or the beginning of a thought that could, one day, be art. Or it was a symbol of personal growth, a touchstone of my development as a person who was no longer actively seeking out ways to feel bad about myself, looking, instead, objectively at a drawing I posted that somehow elicited an emotional reaction from my sister. A drawing that had touched a nerve. The venue through which I could reach her.

But no, it was clear I wasn't going to be Jenny's savior. No manner of tamping down my own happiness or realistically drawing trees would ever help her. Nothing I did would ever mean anything to her.

I texted Jenny: *Can I have my $800 back?*

Looking at it more, my ficus drawing started to feel symbolic of a longing for connection so deep and horrifying that I'd wanted to create an artificial bond with a tree I'd never paid much attention to days before I left it forever. I didn't care about the tree. I didn't care about leaving this specific apartment. I feared leaving things behind only because I feared moving forward. I feared finding myself somewhere else and having to figure out who I was there. I didn't have to be the person I had always been. God, I hated symbolism.

"Would you two be interested in doing some window paintings for the store, perchance?" Cecily asked me and Diana. "I want to take full advantage of employing such talented artists."

"Of course," Diana said. "Use us."

"I'm thinking something summery," Cecily said. "Picnic basket, bottle of white wine, some kind of floral arrangement, charcuterie, one of our woven hats . . ."

"Yeah, sounds good," I said.

"Perfect."

Ah yes, an elevated picnic basket–themed window art triptych. Just a normal average thing one does at one's retail gig.

"Is this real life?" I said.

Diana smiled easily and spun around with an armful of artisanal linen napkins like it was already summer.

"It's our twenties, baby," she said.

With four days left before my *Rushmore* project was due, I felt more detached from the project than ever. I was ready for summer in San Francisco. To live and work with Diana. A tentatively planned road trip to Santa Cruz with Diana in Suz's car. But I still had about half the filming to do, and all of the editing. It would be a joyless thing to carry out, I knew.

I doubted if this defeated, bored feeling was how most artists felt about their work just before finishing it.

I could see from the small piece of window that wasn't covered by curtains that it was pouring rain, so I would have to finish up indoors. Which was a relief, logistically. I never felt comfortable setting the camera up somewhere in public and then performing in front of it. I thought people would look at me, or steal the camera I had rented from the school's tech closet.

If I finished this project, no matter how shitty it turned out to be, I would pass my class. If I didn't, if instead I, say, spent time on my Drawing II final that was due later this week instead, something I understood the point of and found interesting, I would not pass my film class. And if I did not pass my film class, an elective, something that nobody told me I needed, that I enrolled in voluntarily because Suz told me she was taking it, a medium I knew I would never attempt again, I would have to make the credits up another semester. Taking six courses in one semester would be too much, especially if I was to continue working, which I would need to do to stay in San Francisco. If I took six classes, I wouldn't have time to do any projects properly, and I would only turn out more and more shit, rendering my entire skill set and portfolio garbage upon graduation. I wasn't sure how I would be able to rationalize continuing to make art if I couldn't manage to make anything I liked in the four years I'd set aside just for making art. So I would quit art, probably, because what else do you do when you realize you're not good at something? I would quit art, and the only part of my life where I liked who I was would be over.

A fact of my life: I simply had to finish my impossibly shitty film project that didn't make any sense and that absolutely no one cared about. Everything I liked about my life depended on it.

I had chosen, every day of my life thus far, since it came out (not sure when), not to see *Rushmore*. Some days I didn't want to see it. Some days I wanted to be a person who hadn't seen it (which was different). Most days I wasn't thinking about it at all. For some reason, I had wanted having not seen it to mean something. I wanted my rejection of *Rushmore*, my ignorance to it, to be meaningful.

I wanted impossible things. The love of a sister. A friend who was mine alone. Someone to tell me what to do every moment of my life, to take my hands in theirs and manipulate them so that my hands did the things that hands were supposed to do, without my having to learn what that was or how to do it by myself. Tell me what to make and I will make it. Tell me what to be and I will be it. Do I love Picasso? Do I despise Wes Anderson? Do I start saving money so I have something to give Brian someday?

Every decision felt like it was to be engraved on a plaque to be placed under a statue commemorating my shittiness, a long list of bad traits under an emboldened title: WE KNOW WHAT YOU'RE THINKING AND YES THIS GIRL SUCKS. I spent years of my life thinking this way and was just in this moment starting to realize how self-important that was. Nobody was watching me, waiting to see what I did. There weren't any answers to steal. I didn't have to be good or bad or an artist or a genius and I didn't have to decide anything right now. All I had to do right now was make the terrible art I said I was going to make. Integrity was something I could offer the world, even if I had nothing else. Even if I didn't know who I wanted to be. I should just do it so it could be done.

I set up the tripod, pressed the record button, sat down on my bed in front of the camera, and began flatly delivering lines.

Rushmore (2011 Joelle Berry remake)

I am sitting on a bed poorly made up right before filming started, with a blue comforter purchased from Target the year before and a smaller Shrek blanket thrown over the top. There is a pillow under the bed, and this is visible in the frame. I take a moment to get into character, then I look directly into the camera and start speaking.

Me: Here I am in class. Math, I think. I got into this prep school somehow and I'm good at a lot of things. I want to be a great playwright. You might recognize me from other Wes Anderson movies or from being the drummer in the band that did that song "California." I've spent months thinking about the fact that I am going to deliver these lines to you, and zero time thinking about what these lines should be or mean. I've had a lot of other things on my mind, too, and having a lot of thoughts complicates the thinking process. There is a part of me that expects to fail at everything I do, maybe even wants to fail because then I don't have to reorient myself. But then another part of me thinks that I have some hidden innate artistic power that is waiting to be uncovered. And it feels like I'm fighting myself constantly, telling myself I am bound to fail, but pushing on because I'm pretty sure I won't fail. It doesn't seem like other people have this problem, this constant back-and-forth from within. And I keep focusing on things that are out of my control and worrying about them and wasting all my time on that, which drains me, and then I don't have the energy to focus on things I do have control over, like this project, this play I guess, that I'm writing, within this movie. None of this is what I want to say. I'm going to start the next scene.

The next scene begins without so much as a pause.

Me: Okay. Here I am in the next scene. I'm friends with Bill Murray. And the thing with Bill Murray is that we're in love with the same woman. And I think, because I am me and not Bill Murray, that I am the one who deserves to date her. This scene is about being a person who you don't know if you want to be. It's hard to put that feeling into words, so instead of explaining it I will stand near Bill Murray and feel inadequate.

I stand up and, finding that there is no Bill Murray to stand next to, pretend that I have some other reason for standing up.

Me: But I am, you must remember, Jason Schwartzman, born in Hollywood, a relative to the Coppolas, privileged in almost every way. You must remember my lucky life every moment of this film. Every setback and embarrassment I convey is just an act, not the real me. In real life, I do not know discomfort.

It was another one of those gorgeous days where you couldn't tell where the clouds ended and smog began. I took the bus to school, a two-dollar luxury I hadn't allowed myself since the beginning of the semester. I took out my sketchbook and drew bus passengers. My sketchbook pages had already been turned in and graded, so this was just for me. I allowed myself to be looser, sloppy even, making shorthand marks for eyes and laugh lines and jaws. People blended into other people as they departed the bus or I changed focus. The page started to feel alive, filled with stories you'd never know, emotional in that suppressed way that happens on the bus. How interesting it is to be a person. How unknowable you are to everyone else. A face was a way to feel connected within the unknowability. Certain expressions could make you believe you knew exactly what that person felt, what their nature was, whether or not you could trust them. But of course a face doesn't mean any of that. It has no special access to what is beneath it. It is just flesh over bone.

As my stop approached, I considered staying on, continuing my drawing, seeing where the bus went after campus. But I pulled the cord to indicate I wanted the bus to stop for me. I gathered my things back into my backpack, retrieved my bike from the front of the bus, and walked toward Diana and Suz's apartment.

Diana poked her head out from her bedroom window as I called her from the sidewalk below. Her arms locked at the elbow creating a vertical line at the perfect center of the window, her blond hair, normally held together tightly in a ponytail, loose and blowing freely into and out of her face. I wanted to tell her to stay just like that, get my supplies out and draw her.

She gathered all her hair in one hand and held it at her neck.

"I'll be right down," she yelled to me.

I acted on my urge and got my sketchbook out, quickly tried to draw what I remembered of Diana leaning out of her window. Diana emerged from the front door in less than a minute, holding her bike over her shoulder. She locked the door behind her.

"Isn't Suz coming?" I said.

"She said she'd meet us for dinner," Diana said. "She has to prepare some materials for her residency."

After a couple of hours of biking through Golden Gate Park, Diana and I stopped at some grass, laid our bikes down, and ate the sandwiches and fruit we had brought along in our backpacks.

"I loved your piece in that group show," I said.

"Oh, the printmaking show?"

"Yeah, I guess so. It was a while back."

"I found my old diaries last year and felt this flood of memories and nostalgia for being a little kid, and how simple everything was and yet how complicated it all felt. I guess because there are so many layers of meaning and intention in adult lives and as a kid you're trying to parse it all out and make sense of it with your little kid brain. But I don't know, I don't think my prints were super-effective in getting that feeling across."

"No, I felt all of that," I said. "There is a very specific feeling when you're young and just starting to understand attraction but you still believe in cooties and you can't decide which concept is more important."

We sat together quietly. There was a line of trees in front of us and a flat mat of fog behind them, making the space feel tight and two-dimensional, like a backyard on *The Sims*. I knew the city was out there but the details were irrelevant at the moment. It occurred to me that Diana wasn't hanging out with anyone else on her birthday, just me.

"Can I draw you?" Diana said.

"Oh," I said. "Okay."

"You don't have to let me just because it's my birthday," she said.

"No, that's fine. Sure."

I had never posed for a drawing before. I stayed very still even as she was digging supplies out of her bag, wanting to be captured in the moment of being asked to be drawn. I positioned my gaze out above the trees into the fog and imagined the lines of my own face. Diana moved pen across paper, scratching lines representing what I presumed to be my forehead, nose, the way my eyelids disappeared into brow flesh when I was looking upward like this. I felt each scratch vibrate softly through my body. I could feel the flicks of her eyelashes in my skeleton as she looked up at me and then back down at her paper. Her sharp inhales as she considered the next lines like string pulled from behind my ears. People who did torture should try this instead, I thought, because I would've told her anything.

Suz canceled right before we were supposed to meet up for dinner. Diana was unbothered, content to hang out with only me. We went to a strip mall restaurant with absolutely no décor and zero other customers and ordered boba tea and chicken pho and tofu vermicelli.

"That's a cute illustration of a dog," Diana said, pointing to a curly black hair stuck in between the menu and its plastic pocket.

"It reminds me of something my sister would draw," I said.

"Is your sister an artist, too?" she said.

"No." I shook my head and sucked in several boba balls as punctuation. I had surprised myself by bringing up Jenny, and wanted the topic to disappear without further attention. Diana continued looking at me, in a way that made me think she was not only waiting for me to say more, but genuinely wanted me to.

"She's kind of a mess, actually," I said. "She was missing most of this semester. Probably fucked-up on drugs. Left her kid behind and everything. Our mom almost lost her job. I had to send them money for bail. It almost broke our family."

"Oh shit. Wow. Where was she? Is she okay?"

"Who even knows. She's back now. That's kinda just what she does."

Diana nodded and became silent. I realized the gravity of what I'd revealed. This was someone I had to live and work with all summer. This wasn't a relationship I should casually destroy with the messy details of my dramatic personal life. I looked into my noodles desperately. I considered laughing and pretending that it was all a joke. My sister wasn't a drug addict. It was a joke. Ha! It was funny because of how awful it would be if it were true. Haha!

"I had a friend kind of like that in high school. Well, she was my friend since we were really little but she started acting out in high school. She'd always cause the most unnecessary drama, run away from home, try to hide out at my house and force me not to tell anyone, even my parents, then get caught on video stealing from the gas station and the cops would come over and question me about it like I was involved. She didn't have children though. That must have been intense."

I swear the restaurant turned on extra lights or something.

"How is she now?" I said.

"Oh, you know. A little better. She's always in and out of these horrible relationships. There's still constant drama. It's a relief, honestly, to live so far away from her now. In a weird way I always felt responsible for her. I thought I needed to figure out why these things were happening and find a way to help her. Now that I have some distance I realize that kind of help wasn't even something she necessarily wanted from me."

"It's hard to accept that you can't make choices for other people," I said.

"I find it freeing to realize you have to let other people make their choices," she said. "There is no other way."

It started to rain as we walked our bikes home, thick noncommittal drops meant only to scare tourists. But this was our city. This was our day. I took my sweater off and held it over my head. Diana swung around a streetlight pole several times dramatically. She grabbed the sweater off my head, put it on her own, and said, "It's not personal, it's business."

"*The Godfather*?" I said, recalling the line from *You've Got Mail* when Tom Hanks's character said it and then explained that it was a *Godfather* quote.

"*You've Got Mail*," Diana said.

Suz was at the apartment when we got back, wearing a dripping-wet red-and-pink raincoat.

"Sorry I missed everything," she said. "But I got us a present."

She held out a baggie filled with dirt clumps.

"Mushrooms," she said. "Magic kind."

I looked at Diana, who was nodding and smiling and looking textbook appreciative. I wondered if she was actually excited about the drugs or was still in a good mood from the birthday festivities or just didn't know how else to respond to receiving a birthday gift. I should have gotten her something.

Suz opened the bag and put a pinch in each of our palms.

"Right now?" I said.

"Oh, I mean. I'm down. We don't have to, though. I thought it would be a fun birthday thing," Suz said.

"We were thinking of going to karaoke," I said. I looked at Diana to gauge what she was thinking. She shrugged in a way that made me think she wanted to do the mushrooms.

"We totally don't have to," Suz said, noticing my apprehension.

Diana looked at me, waiting for my opinion. I thought a bunch of things at once: Not every decision in my life was in direct response to my sister's poor choices. I didn't have to be perfect, or even good.

Nothing mattered. Vincent van Gogh did drugs and that turned out fine. The mushrooms were free. I could start with a little. The worst thing that could happen is I would die of hypocrisy.

"Okay. Let's do it," I said.

"I'm not feeling anything," I kept saying, unsure if I was relieved or annoyed, until, finally, I stopped having reason to say it.

The world slowly came into more focus, not visually, but with an all-encompassing clarity that washed over all the things in Suz and Diana's apartment. The way art was hung made perfect sense. The smells made perfect sense. (Picture me smelling my own armpit and fully feeling, in the deepest core of my body, that life couldn't sustain itself without armpit smell.) I understood the way I felt about all things without having to bring them up in my mind individually. Everything was just sitting there allowing me to understand it.

"Shit," I said.

Suz sat in a dark corner with a journal, rapidly making pencil marks and turning pages. I said, "Suz," several times and she didn't look up. I wondered if I was only saying her name to myself inside my mind, so I said her name again while looking in a mirror to make sure my mouth moved when I said it. It did, and Suz looked up at me briefly, said nothing, then went back to her journal.

"Can I give you the tour?" Diana said, gesturing to the apartment I'd visited a hundred times.

"I've been here," I said.

"But it's different now that you live here," she said. I could see clearly that she loved me.

Knowing I had visited so many times, and being high herself, she focused on the minute details I may not have picked up on: small irregularities in the wall paint, a doorknob she found special for reasons she couldn't quite verbalize, a window that doves often perched outside of, the kitchen sink, which she called "the most average sink in the hemisphere. So average it should be in a museum."

"Why isn't it in a museum then?" I said.

"Total mystery."

I felt proud. Proud of both of us, for our special bond with the sink (mine developing) but also for the personalities we were forging, for our being able to appreciate objects that people might not normally think anything about. I felt a unique bond growing between me and Diana, one that started with our appreciation of the sink but extended to the fundamental truths of our natures. I could feel our friendship extending itself into the future, inevitable. Then Diana turned the faucet on and we watched water go down the drain for an indeterminable amount of time.

"Suz," I said. I wanted her to share the faucet experience with us. She didn't make any indication that she heard me.

This perfectly captured Suz's entire personality, I thought. Such extreme focus that blocked the rest of the world out. She isolated herself with her work. She retreated inward, into art and books and achievements. When she came out of her bubble it was with intention—to make connections, to gather resources, to soak in the experiences of the world rapidly so she could retreat inward again. She didn't need relationships the way I needed them. She didn't need anything she couldn't provide for herself. If Diana and I weren't here, she'd have other friends. If she didn't have Freddie, there would be some other guy. Or there wouldn't be, and that would be fine for her, too. She didn't need to tie herself to other people for her life to be meaningful. She had herself, she had her art and her ideas and her notebooks, and that was enough for her.

"Isn't this *so* Suz?" I said.

This made Diana laugh hysterically, and then, wiping tears from her eyes, she said, "Yes. This is exactly her."

The way she agreed by phrasing it differently made me think she hadn't understood what I meant, had interpreted it as *Isn't this very much Suz sitting here?* rather than *Doesn't Suz's behavior right now represent everything there is to know about her?*

I tried to clarify, "She doesn't care about anything but herself."

Some of Diana's hair had come out of her ponytail, and she pushed a few of these long blond segments behind her ears. She got a serious look on her face.

"She's got a lot to live up to," she said, looking me right in the eyes, as if she were telling me an important secret.

I didn't know what she meant and felt stupid. I took it personally at first, wondering if it took extra strength for Suz to be my friend, if I needed too much from her, if it was hard to live up to the level of friendship and loyalty I wanted from her. Then I thought it probably had nothing to do with me, that Diana only meant that Suz's family was pressuring her in some way to do well. That her mom, being in the art world herself, had made Suz feel that being a great artist was the only way to impress her. But Suz *was* a great artist, so what could she not be living up to? Because she didn't see how good she was, or she did know but didn't feel it was a firm enough part of her identity? She needed to capture her genius, hold it tightly, squeeze it until more came out.

Or maybe she was not a genius after all. I had thought *she must be a genius* from the moment I met her and had not questioned the notion since, but I also believed I was an unrelenting moron, and if that was true, then that meant I could be wrong about Suz.

As I stared at Suz, the space between us expanded into an impassable gulf, not just physically but spiritually also, whatever that meant. *You're high*, I reminded myself. But it didn't shake the earnestness of the feeling. The gulf was really there. Suz was way over there and I was all the way over here.

It felt okay to see the gulf, to feel it all around me. I didn't have to do anything about it. I realized I had been trying to bridge it, move toward it, extend my arms far enough to fill it, and I was exhausting myself. I didn't need to tie myself to Suz any more than I needed to tie myself to Jenny or my mom or anyone else. They were not me. I'd had this feeling my whole life that the people I spent my time with made me who I was. But now I had the feeling that the opposite was true. I was just myself.

Suz looked up at me with an intensity that normally would have agitated me. *What is she thinking about?* I would have worried. *Something she can't talk about with me because I'm not smart enough to understand.* But tonight I smiled at my pretty friend, her thick bangs cut roughly just above the line of her eyebrows, her mouth pursed in concentration. How lucky I was to know her, to watch her succeed, to have her number show up at the top of my contact list because I called her more frequently than anyone else. What she got from my friendship I wasn't sure. But that was for her to know.

I woke up feeling like my life was over, but in a good way. Like there was some option better than life. I was home, in my own bed, which confused me at first. But then I remembered leaving Suz and Diana's, them pleading with me to stay but leaving anyway, excited to be by myself. I remembered walking through the Castro and buying a cookie. I remembered walking past a grocery store and feeling something profound about the darkened market, deciding it was love that I felt. Broad, directionless love. I walked past Taqueria Cancun and felt the same feeling, though I was less sure it was love this time. Everything seemed to have new paint.

I looked at my phone, seeing notifications for several texts.

Mom: *Im going to pay you back Joey ok*

Mom: *don't harass Jenny for the money things were starting to settle and now shes upset again and taking it out on me and Brian I hate to think of how she acts with brian when I'm at work*

Mom: *I'll send $50 next week ok don't be an asshole.if Jenny leaves again I swear to christ I will drop brian off with you and you can figure it all out this time I cant do it*

Mom: *can you please call Jenny and tell her you were joking about the money*

Diana: *Did you make it home?*

I texted Diana: *Yes! How are you feeling?*

I texted Mom: *ok. Not gonna talk to jenny rn tho*

I took a hot shower, using up the last little bit of a lavender body wash I'd been saving because I didn't want to throw the bottle away. I washed my hair and face and brushed my teeth and flossed. I conditioned my hair and slowly combed it out. After the shower, I moisturized, which I hadn't done in months. I sat on the floor and rubbed lotion into my skin using small circular motions, and my skin soaked it in thirstily. It took a long time, but I got every curve and corner. By the time I stood up, the fog had disappeared from my mirror and my reflection startled me, like someone had been watching me this whole time.

I needed to work on *Rushmore*.

In the art school pamphlets, there were photos of supposed current students in front of canvases and behind computers, in denim jackets with gauged ears and funky glasses, standing close together talking to each other in large open spaces, using hand gestures to make important points, laughing together in gratitude at the shared experience of being an art student. Though I had left the pamphlets in Lodi, I could still see these photos in my head. I had imagined lives and personalities for them. I was intimidated by some and felt attracted to others, but I had imagined all of them to be great artists trying so hard to be even better. I'd had such warmth toward all these imaginary people. Such tenderness.

I had about twenty hours before my class presentation. I felt calm.

I went out to get a breakfast sandwich and found myself wandering into a plant store. I realized what I was doing only as I walked through the door, *ding ding* went the store bell, as if I were a character in a video game and my decisions were being made by some omnipotent force. I walked down the center aisle, wanting to leave but feeling like I owed it to the store to stay. I touched various leaves as I passed them, until something broke off in my hand and, tucking it into the soil of a random plant, I decided not to touch anything else.

Soon it would all be over. *Rushmore* and the semester and my expensive studio apartment would all be behind me. Soon, because these things were over, I would be a different person. Summer would end and I'd have to find another place to live and the fall semester would start up and my job wouldn't last forever or I'd want to find something that suited me better. But soon I would be able to breathe. I would be able to save money, see the numbers in my account slowly getting bigger rather than smaller. Or at least stay the same. I could try to find a cheaper place for the fall, try to work enough hours during the semester that I wouldn't have to take out loans to pay my rent. Things could be different.

"Can I help you find anything?" a petite woman in a floral apron asked.

"Just looking," I said, though I realized when I said it that I wasn't even really looking, was existing fully inside my head, registering nothing that came before my eyes as individual objects, but rather a blur of silver shelving and green life. I decided to look, consciously and fully. I breathed in the potting-soil air, watched light from the window flicker through the leaves of a fern. There was a cat lying on a rag rug in the sun. Greeting cards for sale near the register. A small painted sign advertising 50 percent off succulents.

I bought a purple flower-shaped succulent in a small terra-cotta pot, believing succulents were hard to kill. I would bring it to my new home, put it in the window beside Suz's bed, be a person who had a plant. But first I would bring it to McDonald's, because I still needed breakfast.

integrity definition

was michelangelo crust punk	history
unsocialized weirdo vs eccentric artist	history
what software to use to edit digital footage	history
figure drawing club san francisco	history
diarrhea 4 days	history
best value charcoal pencils	history
how old is diego luna	history

close

At home I felt an urge to start packing. I didn't have any boxes, but I could use some garbage bags to store my clothes and make it easy to transfer them to Suz and Diana's apartment. I could put my old IKEA dresser on the sidewalk for someone to take. I could pack and clean for an hour or two and then work on *Rushmore* . . .

I tried to imagine how I would feel tomorrow, after *Rushmore* was done, after my presentation was over and I could finally move on with my life. I tried to conjure the relief I'd feel then and experience it now, use it as inspiration to finish the project. But I couldn't imagine anything outside of this moment. I was still stuck in this day, and it was only 2:00 p.m., and I still hadn't started working, and I was getting hungry again.

My memory of the few *Rushmore* scenes I had already filmed made me cringe. I couldn't imagine showing them to my class, or having to watch them myself. My voice saying things Catie had said to me. My pathetic costume changes and adjustments to my bedroom to make it look like different scenes. Painful to even remember.

It was all stupid. Going through with a stupid idea made me stupid. I had tried to make myself believe that going through with my stupid idea was smart, because if/when I finished, I could continue school normally and not have to make up extra credits and further diminish my creative time next semester. But that was just an intellectual trick. Finishing it was a stupid waste of my life and not worth the time I was putting into it. It wasn't even worth using the next few hours assembling something incoherent just to have something to turn in.

I emptied my dresser drawers onto the floor and sat among my crap, trying to summon the motivation to carry my dresser down to the sidewalk. I tried to sort things but kept getting confused about what piles were what. Then I decided it was time for more food so I stuffed my crap back into the drawers and left my apartment in search of gas station taquitos.

In *Shrek*, as Shrek and Donkey approach a castle surrounded by a moat of molten lava that they must cross using a tiny bridge, Donkey hesitates and Shrek says, "Oh, you can't tell me you're afraid of heights."

Donkey says, "No, I'm just a little uncomfortable about being on a rickety bridge over a boiling lake of lava."

When I was little I always thought, why couldn't the movie end there? Why couldn't fear of death be a good enough reason to say no? What if Donkey made the decision to trust his intuition, protect himself, turn around and not face the deadly bridge, do something quiet and safe with his life, even if it might seem ordinary to others? Why was the movie teaching me that risk of physical harm should not dissuade me from following through with a plan?

But I was older now, and wiser, and I knew that whatever effects the subliminal messaging in *Shrek* had on me could not be undone, that they could never be understood or quantified. But pondering them years later as a way of procrastinating working on my college assignments was evidence of the ways Donkey had shaped me into a person more willing to kick and scream backward into the inevitable future than to just turn around and do the thing.

I took the battery out of my rental camera to charge it. I breathlessly deleted all the recordings I had already made for *Rushmore* from my computer. Nothing I created in the next twelve hours could be worse than what I had already created. I purged it all: purged my conversations with Catie, purged the scenes I had re-created in my bedroom, purged any preconceived idea of what this film was going to be.

Professor Herrera turned off the classroom light and I pressed play on the DVD I had burned just a few hours earlier.

The film opens to me sitting in my apartment on my bed. The overhead light is off and the small lamp by my bed (off-screen) creates dramatic and mysterious lighting.

Me, reading from a sheet of paper: All my life, I've been defined by my having never seen the movie *Rushmore*. Obviously that is a gross exaggeration. A lie, really. Nobody cares what I've seen. I just needed an opening line. I've been thinking about *Rushmore* pretty much every day for months. I keep asking myself what it's about while avoiding any possible place I might get a legitimate answer. Instead, I've looked for the answer in places where I knew I wouldn't find it.

I continue reading from my notes but ad lib additional words and pause longer than normal between sentences, as it has become clear that the notes I've prepared won't take more than two or three minutes to read, and my film has to be at least twenty minutes long.

Me: I could easily watch *Rushmore*. It feels like a metaphor for every precarious thing in my life. How easy it would be to destroy any integrity I have by watching this DVD [I pick up a DVD case that is sitting beside me and place its cover in front of the camera lens] purchased for three dollars from the movie rental place I like that's going out of business. I've manufactured a life for myself in which it feels like a betrayal to my artistic identity to watch an old DVD. But since nobody cares, that means ultimately my artistic integrity is just what I think of myself. And the meaning of art is what the viewer thinks it means. Art is about what you think the world is about, or what you think your life is about, or what you think is important to think about. You probably already know that, but I'm learning it now. *Rushmore* is the most impactful movie of my life because I've decided that it is. Arbitrarily. I've never seen Wes Anderson's version, but this is mine.

That's all of my notes, but I continue holding the paper up in front of me. I thought I might be able to improvise more material, but now that it is time to improvise I can't think of anything else to say. For a few moments I am motionless, my eyes fixed on the sheet of notes that I have already read in their entirety. I'll need to stop filming, write more notes, and start again.

Impulsively, I decide to leave the apartment. My brain is still process- ing the idea as my body jumps into action. There is no plan after "leave the apartment," but this is what my body is doing, so I go with it. My brain will come up with some reason for doing all of this at some point. With one hand (still filming myself with the other) I gather everything I might need: my computer, the camera bag with the cables I need to connect it to my computer, some cables I'm not sure I need because I don't know what they're for, my copy of Rushmore so I still have the option to sabotage my integrity later, extra socks, a single bagel in a paper bag, a jar of peanut butter, and a spoon. I put everything in my backpack, put my backpack over my shoulder, and grab my keys from the shelf by the door. The footage is rocky as I fumble with my keys outside my apartment door and walk out onto the street. I hold the camera in front of me but am too embarrassed to put my arms up enough to get a good angle, so what is filmed is a low, unflattering angle of mostly my neck and the underside of my jaw. The camera autofocuses in and out on my head, a blur of dark blue sky and bright yellow lights and the faint outlines of buildings behind me. Once I get onto the main street, I gain some courage. You can see, in the film, tension release from my face. I lift the camera up for a straighter shot. I start running down Eighteenth. I simply trust my body to go where it wants to go. Where this sense of trust comes from, I don't know. I am a deeply distrustful person, always afraid of being duped or buying in at the wrong moment. I still haven't made the move from boot cut to skinny jeans, for example. I pass a bar and someone standing outside the bar next to a sign that reads improv comedy show yells, "The funniest night of your life is starting in five minutes." I pretend I don't hear them and they yell, "Guess you don't like to have fun, you sick fuck." I pass another bar and two people I recognize from school but have never talked to are standing outside. I angle the camera more toward the street so they are not in the background of my footage. I cross Valencia. I cross Mission, slowing down because there are other people around and I need to weave carefully through them. I'm turning down Sixteenth. Something falls onto the lens and blocks part of the image for around a minute, then disappears on its own, revealing that I am still running, eyes fixed ahead. It is during this time that I realize where I am going. I do not have to change direction, as my body seems to have known the whole time. The number of hours I have left to edit this film are becoming few. I step right into a puddle, soaking my left foot. I can remember the first time I went downtown after I moved to San Francisco, how the tall ornate buildings made me feel historic. Things had happened here to other people and they would happen to me, too. In Lodi nothing ever happened to anyone, except for once in a while someone's friend from Truckee would come to town and insist on Jell-O shots in Dixie cups and everyone would have to throw down five dollars to make it happen to please this Truckee person. I think it would be nice if not every single thing that happened to me turned into an emotionally complex personality-defining event I'd have to carefully decode for years to come. I think that would be very pleasant. I am suddenly aware of how awful my face looks every moment of this film and, being that the film is almost entirely my face, feel embarrassed that my classmates will see me like this. This is mixed with a sort of pride for being confident and brave enough to look this ugly on-screen. I am so proud of my gross face. I think about slowing down and speaking into the camera again. There needs to be something more to say. Rushmore needs more dialogue. But I don't want to say anything. I don't speak. I get everything I want. I always have. It starts to rain, and I am a little afraid that the camera will be destroyed by water and I will have to pay for it. Then it quickly stops raining and what I worry about is whether or not the camera has enough battery life to get me where I'm going so this can all be one shot. Everyone in class should know where I am at this point. Some of them have passed these spots many times themselves. I am panting so heavily you can no longer hear my footsteps. It occurs to me only now, in watching, that I never show what I'm running toward, only what is behind me. I fear there are metaphors here that I don't intend. Something I find interesting about San Francisco is that I live here. It is a city everybody knows and I get to be a part of it. The light and the fog and the cool summers are part of my story. Sometimes I pick a random window from a grid of windows on a building in a sea of buildings and try to imagine what interpersonal dramas they are facing. A cheating spouse. A child who has been bullied at school and escapes in video games. Two people fighting a silent fight about their romantic intentions. An expectation of sex. Ugly words spoken in an order calculated to devastate. An episode on TV that has been seen millions of times by millions of people but is new to this particular person. A baby crying while his mom is in the shower. We are all here together. I always get the things I want. I've been living my life like that's a bad thing. I get everything I want and I guess part of what I want is to feel bad all the time. Some people are given everything in their lives. Then they are given, on top of everything else, the freedom of not doubting whether they deserve it. Two nights before, I went on the Verizon website (instead of working on this project) and blocked Jenny's number and then, a few minutes later, unblocked it. Deep down inside I care only about myself. I am looking tired now, and sweaty. I'm not used to running. In class, I am wearing the same clothes I wore in the film, and my hair is in the same loose, greasy ponytail, making abundantly clear that this project was made extremely last-minute. If I am ever asked, I will tell the truth and say I do not know what art is. In the background of the film the campus parking lot becomes visible, and then the large nondescript building in front of the main campus build-ing is visible, and anyone in class will now know where I am, will have made these same steps after me today. I wonder if I should have run someplace else. Maybe to the ocean, another thing I've never seen despite my lifelong proximity. Another choice, a series of choices, a lifetime of the same choice that feels like no choice at all. Making art is my way of tricking myself into believing that the past is something I can continue shaping. It would have taken me a lot longer to run to the ocean, but I could have done it. I could have walked right up to the ocean, famous for being huge and mysterious, and recorded what it looked like spilling between my fingers. I slow to a walk for the final few yards to the school entrance, breathing loudly into the camera's built-in mic. I stand in front of the door to the main building of my school and search my bag for my identification card, which lets me into the building after 10:00 p.m. I find it and wave myself through the machine. Hello, I belong here. Once I am inside I become self-conscious of filming myself again. There are more people in the building than there usually are at this time. It's finals for everybody, I realize, not just me. There are a few moments of footage of me looking around, disoriented, my brain trying to come up with a plan now that we are here, like, Where would be good to sit down and make sure my foot-age has been properly recorded, *and* Do I need some specific soft-ware to finish this project, *but these moments don't make it into the final cut. Rushmore ends in the entrance hall, where almost two years ago I entered for the first time and wrote my name on the sign-in sheet for freshman orientation, feeling like I had fallen into someone else's life. It is a line right through the past and present. A dot on the map that made my whole life different forever. The screen goes black and my classmates remain silent, as if more might be coming, but that is it. That is the end. That's what I've made. I have done it. I am done.*

I watched my classmates regain control of their faces as the lights turned back on. I blinked, hyperaware of how my eyelids felt smacking together, separating, smacking together again. They quickly started discussing the film, not, I assumed, because my work stirred something in them that they needed to try to put into words, but because class participation made up 30 percent of our final grade.

Suz smiled at me from across the room and I smiled back. The gulf between us hadn't disappeared. In fact, it seemed even more impenetrable now. How far away she looked. How unknowable. How okay I actually was with that.

Acknowledgments

Thank you, Kendall Storey.

Thank you, Monika Woods.

Thank you, Artist Trust and Spokane Arts.

Thank you, Jillian Weise, Sharma Shields, Elle Nash, Juliet Escoria, Elizabeth Ellen, Chloe Caldwell, Elliot Reed, Margaret Starry, and Mallory Moore.

Thank you, Yuka Igarashi, Wah-Ming Chang, Michael Salu, Mikayla Butchart, Megan Fishmann, Lena Moses-Schmitt, Rachel Fershleiser, and everyone else at Soft Skull.

Thank you, Sherrie Amberson and Andie Cohen.

Thank you, Ian and Casper.

CHELSEA MARTIN is the author of the essay collection *Caca Dolce* and the novella *Mickey*, among other books. She lives in Spokane, Washington, with her husband and child. Find out more at www.cacadolce.com.